THE

TYRANT'S

DAUGHTER

J. C. CARLESON

ALFRED A. KNOPF
NEW YORK

Text copyright © 2014 by J. C. Carleson
Jacket photograph copyright © 2014 by Ilona Wellman/Trevillion Images
"Truth in Fiction" essay copyright © 2014 by Dr. Cheryl Benard

All rights reserved. Published in the United States by Alfred A. Knopf, an imprint of Random House Children's Books, a division of Random House LLC, a Penguin Random House Company, New York.

Knopf, Borzoi Books, and the colophon are registered trademarks of Random House LLC.

Visit us on the Web! randomhouse.com/teens
Educators and librarians, for a variety of teaching tools,
visit us at RHTeachersLibrarians.com

Library of Congress Cataloging-in-Publication Data
Carleson, J. C.
The tyrant's daughter / J.C. Carleson. — First edition.
p.   cm.
Summary: Exiled to the United States after her father, a Middle Eastern dictator, is killed in a coup, fifteen-year-old Laila must cope with a completely new way of life, the truth of her father's regime, and her mother and brother's ways of adjusting.
ISBN 978-0-449-80997-6 (trade) — ISBN 978-0-449-80998-3 (lib. bdg.) — ISBN 978-0-449-81000-2 (ebook) — ISBN 978-0-449-80999-0 (pbk.)
[1. Exiles—Fiction. 2. Immigrants—Fiction. 3. Dictators—Fiction. 4. Middle East—Politics and government—Fiction. 5. High schools—Fiction. 6. Schools—Fiction.] I. Title.
PZ7.C21479Tyr 2014 [Fic]—dc23 2013014783

The text of this book is set in 11-point Galliard.

Printed in the United States of America
February 2014
10 9 8 7 6 5 4 3 2
First Edition

For Kai, who was there for every word

I.

PRETENDING

My brother is the King of Nowhere.

This fact doesn't matter to anyone except my family—a rapidly shrinking circle of people who Used to Be. And, even for us, there are surprisingly few perks. Now we sit in our airless apartment, curtains closed against the outside world, pretending.

My mother pretends that nothing has changed.

She is good at this charade. Her every gesture oozes money and power now long gone. They wouldn't let her take her closets full of designer clothes when we left our country, but she still spends hours on her appearance—pretending that photographers might still want to take pictures of her every outing, even dressed as she is now in J. C. Penney sale-rack clothes and drugstore lipstick. Pretending her old life didn't die along with my father.

My brother is six.

I try to remember six. What it might feel like at that age to be told that you are the exiled ruler. That you deserve to be king. That someday soon you will be—once the right people die, that is.

My younger brother's almost-title and nonexistent kingdom do not make *me* anything at all. And yet I'm right here beside him, thousands of miles from everything I once knew. Mine is a nameless, purposeless banishment. Guilt by relation.

My fifteenth birthday came and went yesterday. No one remembered. It's understandable, I suppose, considering what we've all been through in the last few weeks. There are bigger things to remember, and we all certainly have far bigger things to forget.

Perhaps I'll start calling myself the Invisible Queen. Sometimes just having a title helps.

My brother the king does not like that he has to share a bedroom with me.

I don't like it either. So I pretend he's not there. I ignore his king-sized tantrums and the dirty royal socks that he leaves on my bedspread. I pretend not to hear him when he tells me what to do.

"Mom!" Bastien shouts. "Laila isn't obeying me. Tell her she has to obey. I'm the king!" He pouts in a very regal way.

It doesn't help that Mother encourages him. She thinks it's cute. "Laila. Can't you at least show him respect? Someday you will have to, you know." She pinches his cheeks. "My little prince."

"King!" he insists, getting even more angry. "I'm not a prince. I'm a king!"

I suppose it doesn't occur to him that his promotion from prince came at the cost of our father's life. He's only a child, after all; he can be forgiven for missing the connection. So sometimes I play along. "Yes, Your Majesty." I curtsy, even though back home we never did such things. Ours was not that kind of royalty. Not the kind with ball gowns or high tea or croquet matches played on manicured lawns. It wasn't even real.

But still we pretend.

HINDSIGHT

A memory.

Bastien whining and turning up the volume on the TV. "Daddy, make them stop. I can't hear my show." He keeps pressing the button, up up up, until the voices of the talking cartoon fish drown out the sound of gunfire outside.

Father ruffles Bastien's hair. Confident to the end, if you weren't close enough to see the frown lines around his eyes and mouth growing deeper every day. If you didn't pay attention to how many hours he spent just pacing, pacing. If you didn't notice, as I didn't at the time, that he hardly seemed to leave the house anymore, or that when he did go out, it was with twice as many bodyguards as before. "It's amazing," he says to us. "The satellite dish still works, through it all. Everything else out there has gone to hell, but just look at that resolution. Programs from the other side of the world—the best technology money can buy."

In hindsight, perhaps he should have been paying closer attention to the guns.

Here, now, Bastien and Mother continue to turn the television volume up too high. Blocking out memories, perhaps? Or more likely just habit. Now it only serves the purpose of blocking out the sound of the neighbor in the apartment next door—a cranky old woman living alone who beats against the wall with a broom, or maybe a cane. Something that makes a faint, rhythmic *bang bang bang* sound that is no competition for the sound of bullets flying. No one else in our apartment seems to even hear it.

I turn down the volume when they aren't paying attention, and try to smile in apology when I see the old woman outside. *It's not their fault*, I want to say. But isn't it? What else do they ignore simply because it suits them? What else have we all ignored?

The old woman just glares at me. All she wants is peace and quiet in her shabby apartment, and I can't give it to her. In her eyes, I am useless.

CHOICES

Now we live in not-quite-Washington, D.C. Our home is twenty-five miles away from a capital where we have no status, in a suburb that feels so distant from either past or future that it might as well be on the moon. An exile within an exile.

Nothing is familiar. Nothing is easy. Not even for a King of Nowhere or an Invisible Queen.

At first, the differences between Old Life and New Life were most obvious in the small and the unimportant.

The grocery store, for example. An entire aisle of cereal. Hundreds of boxes. Hundreds of choices. Of course I had eaten cereal before. I'm not a savage. Mother's shopping trips in Europe were always followed a few weeks later by the arrival of wooden crates full of her carefully selected treasures from abroad. Bastien and I would tear at the contents, racing each other for the discovery of the small luxuries Mother had picked out for us, nestled among the bottles of liquor, perfume, and other adult delicacies that didn't interest us in the least. For us there were metal tins of fancy chocolates, giant tubs of peanut butter, comic books, DVDs, and always, always our favorite cereals, which we ate from Grandmother's delicate teacups rather than bowls in order to make each box last one or two more precious mornings.

Cereal was a small, affordable luxury—one we knew well. But it was still a luxury. An effort. A point of pride. Something special, chosen and imported just for *us*. Father's position meant that rules were broken so we might have things that others in our country could not. Those crates of cereal meant that we *deserved* what others did not.

Here, the choices that stand before me in the store aisles seem to exist only to mock me. *Cereal isn't a* luxury, *you stupid fool,* the boxes laugh at me. *You were really impressed by a couple of jars of* peanut butter? Two aisles down I count twenty-seven different kinds of that too. And mustard. Dozens of varieties of mustard.

Is it really necessary?

It makes me angry, all of that mustard. Those taunting boxes of cereal, so overvalued in my memory.

Bastien sees things differently. He squealed and whirled and grabbed the first time he saw that aisle of temptation. He lost himself in the choices, filling our shopping cart until Mother told him, smiling, that that was enough cereal for the moment. He ate himself sick that evening, mixing enormous bowlfuls of cocoa nuggets with marshmallow crisps with honey puffs. I pulled my pillow over my head as the exiled king vomited Lucky Charms all through the night.

9

STANDARDS

The king and I start school.

It's not our choice. Mother didn't like it—none of us were ready for it—but something came in the mail that shook her up enough to change her mind. I only managed to read a few phrases before she snatched the letter away. "Condition of legal immigrant status." "Violation of terms." "Deportation."

Mother seethes enough for all of us. She doesn't like being told what to do. Who do they think they are, sending this threatening, impersonal letter in the mail? Treating us like common immigrants!

It's easier to just obey. Besides, after three weeks of staring at each other in our tiny apartment, we all need a break. Our mourning has kept us docile. Lethargic. But our grief-induced stupor is starting to lift, and we're growing restless and more and more irritable with one another every day. Maybe school is a good thing. Even Bastien is unusually compliant with the idea.

I have one condition.

I want an interpreter. Not for language. For life. Someone who can help me understand cereal aisles and lunch lines and other small, baffling things like the posters in the hallway telling students to wear their pajamas to school for spirit day. MTV and the Cartoon Network, blaring on our television whenever Bastien can seize control of the remote, are only marginally more useful than my mother at explaining these things.

The school is quick to assist. They assign me Emmy, a student mentor. President of the international students club, though she's never been anywhere except Canada and on a weeklong beach vacation at a resort in Mexico. I know because she shows me photos the first time we meet.

I'm embarrassed to say that my first thought when I meet Emmy is a single, ugly word.

Whore.

But it isn't my fault. It isn't my voice. It's the voice of my uncles. All but one are dead now, but they still sometimes speak, cruel and accusing as ever, in my thoughts.

In my country, women wear layers. Our clothing flows and drapes. It hints and implies.

I shouldn't have reacted. I've seen enough television to know how people here dress. That the clothing here shouts. That it confesses secrets that remain better kept elsewhere. I'd seen it for myself in Paris when my mother took me on one of her shopping trips as a birthday treat. She'd boarded the airplane dressed as usual. But each hour, each trip to the first-class restroom, revealed slightly more of her. A scarf removed here. A shawl removed there. By the time we landed, my mother was transformed. Unwrapped.

At the time, I was in awe of the way she'd changed, like a butterfly coming out of a cocoon. And then, on the way back home, I was relieved to see the layers reappear, piece by piece, returning the glamorous stranger in the seat next to mine back into my mother.

But even my Paris mother had limits cheerfully ignored by Emmy, whose bare shoulders display peeling traces of an old sunburn and whose freckled and scratched legs climb alarmingly high until they meet a short skirt at the very last possible moment. That she can feel so at ease in her flawed skin is astonishing to me.

Emmy must feel me looking at her. Judging her. Because her smile stiffens slightly and she takes a small step back, a wounded expression on her face.

I still have power.

But I know that she isn't a whore, or any of the other, even worse things that women are sometimes called in my country. I know that, here, she is perfectly normal. My new normal.

I am the one who has to change. To transform, like my mother on that airplane ride. I offer Emmy a smile and some small talk to make up for my insult.

She accepts, perking up before my eyes. "Wow, you speak English really well," she says, slowly and too loudly.

"I would hope so. I've been tutored in French and English since I was old enough to walk." It is a princess's voice. I see Emmy's face catch that, too. I have to change faster.

"But thank you," I say in a stranger's humble voice. Another apologetic offering.

Forgive me. I'm still learning.

Emmy. So cheerfully American, so wholesome and naïve even in her near nakedness, forgives yet again. I will have to study her carefully. Surely this openness has limits.

OBSTACLES

I wait for Bastien at his bus stop after school, thinking that if his first day was anything like mine, he'll want me there. I'm grateful for the chance to just sit on a bench in silence for a few minutes, since my mind is numb from sensory overload. Hallways full of people wearing impossibly bright, bright colors have left my eyes feeling scorched. Today was a blurred parade of socks that matched shirts that matched sweaters—indulgent color coordination that you only see on pampered children in my country. Toothy white smiles punctuated the faces of the candy-colored strangers in the hallways, leaving me feeling like a small, dark storm cloud skittering grimly from corner to corner.

Bastien is somehow unaffected.

He leaps off the bus looking remarkably like all of the other six-year-olds who tumble out behind him. He's a king disguised as a commoner, right down to the grass stains on his knees and the cowlick in his hair. The only hint of his foreign-ness is the leather satchel he carries—the same one he carried on our rushed flight away from home.

He needs a backpack like the other kids, I see. Something made of cheap nylon, with a superhero emblazoned on it. And bright. It has to be a bright color. I make a mental note to help him buy one. There's no reason that any of this should be harder on him than it needs to be.

"Bastien!" I call out as the other kids push past us. He looks happy to see me. That he looks happy for any reason reassures me. "How was the bus?"

He looks up at me with wide eyes. "The driver stopped for a squirrel!" His voice is full of awe.

I cringe. I know exactly why this should matter to him—why he should find such a thing incredible.

"Everything's different here." It's the only thing I can think to say as I put my arm around his shoulders and hustle him toward home. Luckily my response seems to satisfy him, and he doesn't mention it again. Instead, he chatters happily about recess and fire drills. The memory is roused in my mind, though, and it oozes uncomfortably in my thoughts like a lanced blister.

Bastien is thinking, I know, of a scorching hot day not long ago—another memory from our Before. Our driver was racing through the streets faster than usual. Going anywhere as a family required a cumbersome and cheerless parade of at least five cars. A security detail always rode in the first and the last cars—grim-faced men who carried guns and never spoke to me. The cars in the middle varied in their order. They were identical by design—armored cars shipped in from South Africa that reminded me of heavy, metal armadillos. On this day my parents rode in one car, Bastien and I in another, and the third car was a decoy driven by a nervous chauffeur who took no comfort in being the least valuable member of our bulletproof procession. The position of Father's car changed every time so that no one ever knew which car to attack. We were shuffled around like a deck of cards—the moving target that was my parents' car sometimes ahead of us and sometimes behind. The elaborate vehicular waltz was just one more attempt to fool those who wished us harm.

Bastien and I were stuck riding in the car with the air-conditioning that barely worked. We were sweaty and cranky, and Bastien was whining about not being able to roll down the windows. "They don't open," I explained yet again. "Because of the bulletproofing. It's to keep us safe." I craved fresh air too, though, and I would have happily sacrificed a bit of personal safety for a gust of wind to cool the car's sweltering interior. I had just reached up to push a sweaty piece of hair out of my eyes when the car lurched violently and then sped up even more, tires squealing as the vehicle fishtailed and rocked.

"What's going on? What are you doing?" As my father's daughter, I could speak to the driver with a certain amount of imperiousness.

But the driver was hunched over the wheel, too focused to answer. I whirled around just in time to glimpse what had caused him to swerve.

Out the thick, tinted window, I saw it. Bastien did too.

There was a body in the street.

A man, probably, but it was hard to tell. It was a man-sized heap, anyway, lifeless and crumpled in the middle of the road. I suppose it could have been a person only injured or unconscious, but something about the wretched stillness of the body made me certain that death had long since paid its visit.

But as horrible a sight as it was—a discarded corpse almost close enough to touch—what happened next was worse.

The car behind us—whether my father's car or the decoy even I didn't know—did *not* swerve. It did not veer even an inch to avoid the object in its path.

That car, heavy with its armored plating, drove over the ragged corpse as if it were nothing more than a piece of trash in the road. I heard a thump as it happened, although it was probably only my imagination—my brain giving the gruesome image its own gruesome soundtrack.

I may have imagined the sound of the impact, but I definitely did not imagine the sound of the chief of security shouting, firing the driver on the spot as soon as we pulled into the razor-wire safety of our vacation compound. Our chauffeur, the man who had been white-knuckled with the effort of steering us safe of the terrible obstacle just a few minutes earlier, did not say a word to defend himself. He accepted his punishment with the slumped shoulders of someone who knows he has made an unforgivable mistake.

Only later could I bring myself to ask Father what the driver had done wrong. He frowned when I asked, and looked as if he didn't want to answer. He did answer, though. That was something about my father. He always told me the truth if I asked the right question.

"Laila, dearest, it was a matter of safety." His frown deepened as he chose his words. "There are people who put things in the road to force us to change our course. And then they booby-trap the path that looks safest. Do you understand? A driver who swerves is the driver most likely to trigger a roadside bomb. The protocol is to never deviate from the planned course, no matter what, and your driver violated that protocol. He put you in danger, so he had to be fired."

"But it was a body. A person!" A tear escaped and my voice cracked, causing my father to turn away. He didn't like displays of weakness. I didn't care. Not at that moment, anyway, though normally even the faintest hint of irritation was enough to make me scramble to amend whatever it was I had done to displease him. I didn't want to accept his explanation. I didn't want to live in his world. A world in which windows were sealed shut and bodies were mere bumps in the road. I ran from the room, and we never discussed it again.

But now my six-year-old brother marvels at a bus that stops for squirrels.

Bastien darts away from me, shoving his leather satchel into my hands so that he can run over to the shabby playground across from our apartment. As he scampers toward the rusty swing set, I wonder if he tried the window on the bus. When he found that it would open, how did he react? Was he grateful for the breeze, or was he frightened by the possibility of what dangers could enter along with the wind?

I hope the former, but truly I do not know. We have been shaped differently by our past, Bastien and I.

WORDS

Emmy brings me into her circle of friends, introducing me and showing me off like a shiny new toy. *This is Laila,* Emmy begins each introduction. Depending on the audience, she then sprinkles in little morsels of information about me. *Laila speaks fluent French,* she says in a prideful tone, as if she deserves some credit. Or, *This is Laila's first time in the United States.* Or, sometimes, *She speaks English better than I do!* I am an exotic pet.

Most people are kind. They're friendly in the overwhelming way I'm starting to realize is normal here, and when they smile in that way that makes me think of a tiger's grin, I remind myself that this is what is expected here. I show my teeth back.

The girls at the lunch table are unimpressed, hungry for more interesting morsels than Emmy provides. And Emmy, in turn, is hungry for their approval. She turns defensive when one of the girls, Morgan, questions her.

"What is she, an exchange student or something?" Morgan sniffs, looking more interested in her yogurt than she is in me.

I resist the urge to speak for myself. This is Emmy's show.

"No." Emmy's words sound clipped, sharp. "She lives here now. Permanently. With her family."

One of the other girls—Hailey? Or perhaps Kailee?—stage-whispers something to Morgan. "Ef oh bee."

I don't know what it means, but Emmy reacts. "That is *so* rude! She is *not* an F.O.B." She turns to me to translate. "Fresh off the boat. *Such* a racist thing to say."

Hailey-Kailee-Bailee turns red, chastised.

I am amused. I *am* fresh off the boat—or, more accurately, the chartered plane. I don't see the insult in the statement, though it's clear one is intended. Emmy, however, is offended enough for both of us, and she defends me rapid-fire. "She's *not* an exchange student, and she's *not* an F.O.B. Her family is famous—you'd know if you ever bothered watching the news. Her dad was, like, a *dictator*. He ran the whole country."

The conversation goes on around me, but I freeze at that word.

"You shouldn't have said that," I say as soon as Emmy and I walk away from the lip-gloss tribunal at the lunch table. We'd been judged and found worthy, an invitation to join the girls extended and politely refused in order to continue my public debut. "It isn't true."

"Hmmm?" Emmy is distracted, pleased by her social coup. I have no speaking part in her scripted introductions.

"What you said. About my father. It isn't true." I'm trying

20

to keep my anger in check, but my old voice, the one that used to be obeyed, returns to me unbidden. "Don't say it again."

Emmy reacts to my tone. She looks stricken. The girls at the table were bad enough, and now *I'm* attacking her too. Her exotic pet has claws and teeth. It is too much for her to handle. "B-but," she stammers, "that's what the news said. I looked you up. I read the articles. Your father was in charge, right? I mean, I saw pictures and everything. Your mom is beautiful, by the way."

"He. Was. Not. A. Dictator." It is my turn to say the words slowly and too clearly to be misunderstood.

Emmy is still confused. "But you should be proud, Laila. Your family is famous! You're like royalty or something!"

The distinction is lost on her. "Just don't call him a dictator," I ask softly.

She doesn't want to let it go. Just as I found no harm in *F.O.B.*, she finds no harm in her word. "I'll show you where it says he is. Come over to my house after school. You can see for yourself."

I should say no. I should be confident enough about my father's legacy to refuse—it is an insult to my family to even entertain the idea.

I accept.

INVITATIONS

I can't help but hunch my shoulders against the feeling of being watched. Emmy's bedroom is unsettling.

A hundred sets of eyes stare at me from the walls. It's an amateur portrait gallery—a snapshot collage of faces. Some of the photos—boys only—have *X*'s penned across them. I don't ask why. I already knew that Emmy was a collector of people. I am her latest specimen, after all.

Her mother knocks on the door of her room and asks if I will be staying for dinner. She looks nervous.

"Yes!" Emmy shouts out in answer, then turns to me. "Right, Laila? You can stay, can't you? Please?" I notice that she has angled her body so it's blocking the computer screen.

"Um . . . okay, good. I mean, fine." Her mom's brow is furrowed. "We're having lasagna. Is that okay with you?" She emphasizes her words strangely, as if expecting me to object. "I mean, do you have any—" She searches for the right words,

"Any dietary restrictions? From your country, or your religion?" Just like her daughter, she plays with a golden pendant hanging from her neck. Hers is a small cross.

I suddenly understand her nervousness. "Lasagna sounds wonderful, Mrs. Davis. Thank you very much for the invitation. I would love to stay for dinner."

Emmy's mother's face unfurrows and she smiles broadly, looking so much like her daughter for a moment that it's like seeing double. She is pleased that I have not rejected her food. Would she be so pleased if she could read the pages that her daughter is hiding?

Emmy fidgets and glowers until her mother leaves the room, and then rolls her eyes. "It's probably better my mom not see this stuff. She's *so* controlling." I hide my expression behind my hair. The googling girl with her own computer in her bedroom thinks her mother is controlling.

Emmy's fingers fly over the keyboard as I watch and pretend to be indifferent. Back home we had no internet. Or at least not the internet I see before me now. We had only a heavily censored, filtered version, with threatening messages decrying all but the blandest of government-approved sites as forbidden.

"See?" Emmy asks as she finds what she was looking for. "I didn't make it up. I really am sorry, Laila. I didn't know it would offend you."

I force the corners of my mouth to turn up and form a forgiving expression as I gaze past her to read the headline emblazoned across the screen. The picture that accompanies the article is old, taken several years ago, and my father looks heavier, healthier than I remember from more recent days. My mother is walking behind him in the photo. It is not a flattering image of her, but she is still beautiful, even with her eyes shifted toward something out of camera range. She looks skittish, like a storm-spooked horse, with the whites of her eyes showing too much.

The article on Emmy's computer screen is not kind.

"It's not true." I want to keep reading, but the need to defend is more urgent. I've seen enough to know that whoever wrote the article was wrong, had only part of the story. There are several unattributed quotes that sound suspiciously like things my uncle would say. My uncle, who does not share the blame in this article, but who certainly shares the blame in real life.

Emmy shrugs and begins to braid her hair, checking her progress in the mirror above her dresser. She truly does not care. The accusations on her computer describe events so far away from her they might as well belong in a fairy tale. *Once upon a time, there was an evil man who led his country into war and misery.*

The truth is more Shakespearean tragedy than fairy tale, though. *Upon his death, an emperor's sons vie for power, only to destroy everything around them and pass their bloody quarrel on to the next generation.* Whether fairy tale or Elizabethan tragedy, such stories don't come true in Emmy's world. My life is no more real to her than an assigned reading for English class.

"There's a lot more," Emmy says once her braid is finished. "Do you want to see it?"

Yes.

"No," I say.

"Okay, then let's go eat. My mom's lasagna is awesome, but stay away from her garlic bread. She burns it every time." Emmy is out the door, the article already forgotten.

I glance back at her computer before I follow. I want to read more, but I don't want to read more—conflicting urges grapple in my gut. Either way, I know for certain that I don't want my carefree new American friend looking over my shoulder as I read. Surely the same thought would occur to her as the one that now pulsates and throbs in my head like a malignant tumor, and I couldn't bear the doubled weight of our combined question: *What kind of person doesn't know whether her father was a king or a monster?*

DIRECTIONS

I hurry home after my dinner at Emmy's. The walk is long, but I'm not ready to try the city's bus system. Just looking at the schedule, with its seemingly infinite routes and destinations, makes my head spin.

But even on foot, I'm disoriented within minutes. Not lost, exactly. Not yet. But I'm angry with myself for not paying more attention when I walked here with Emmy. Alone, everything looks different. The cocoon in which I used to live has been ripped away, but that doesn't mean I'm ready to spread my wings. Simply to walk, unaccompanied, from one place to the next is new enough—one part liberation, one part intimidation. The fact that all the buildings look the same to me does not help. How many fast-food restaurants can possibly coexist in one small area?

I turn left at the Golden Arches, only to realize my error a half block later. It should have been a right at the arches and then a left at the sign advertising fried chicken by the bucket—a landmark that never fails to amaze me. Even with my privileged background, I can hardly fathom the food quantities here, measured in buckets, tubs, platters, and combo packs. I backtrack, cursing. No one shoots at me here, and the bumper-sticker-adorned cars are neither armored nor driven by bodyguards, but my heartbeat quickens anyway. There is comfort, if not safety, in familiarity, and nothing here feels familiar.

Finally my apartment building shows itself—a five-story stucco beacon in the dusk. Unbelievably, my home.

Inside, Bastien is eating cereal again—his enthusiasm for it has only grown since we arrived. Mother is painting her fingernails with no evidence of a meal before her. The lasagna sits guiltily in my stomach. It *was* delicious.

"Have you eaten?" I ask.

She beckons me with her fingers extended and spread, her gesture intended both to dry the red paint and to call me over for a kiss on each cheek. "I can't bring myself to eat that sugar-coated Styrofoam your brother is so obsessed with. It tastes like chocolate-dipped mothballs. I'd rather go hungry."

I open the cupboards to confirm what I already know. Nothing but the last two boxes of cereal left from our grand first shopping trip, both nearly empty. I have to bite my tongue to keep from shouting out in frustration. Does it not occur to her to buy anything else? She may not mind going hungry, but couldn't she remember that she has children who will need to eat tomorrow, and the next day, and the next day after that?

Unless there is another reason.

I approach the topic carefully, and only after making a cup of tea, using the last tea bag from a tin I found in the back of an otherwise empty drawer. "I thought you might like some tea," I say as I bring her the offering. I try to think of something bland and nonconfrontational to discuss. In our culture it is considered rude to skip straight to business without first sharing a meal and a conversation. My question keeps bubbling up in my throat, though, growing in urgency until I feel like I might choke. Finally, I can't contain it.

"Are we out of money?" It comes out rushed and petulant, not as I intended. I sound like a child asking an adult question.

"Don't worry, Laila. Money will come." She's too busy inspecting her cuticles to look up at me.

"From where?" I can't let this drop. We can't eat from cereal boxes forever. "Maybe you should get a job."

Mother looks amused. "Doing what, darling? Working behind the counter at the corner gas station, perhaps? Can't you just see it?" She laughs and begins to apply a second coat of polish to her nails.

"Then *I'll* get a job. *I* could work at the gas station. Or I could work as a tutor, maybe." I have no idea how to go about getting a job in this country, or even if anyone would hire a fifteen-year-old immigrant—an *F.O.B.*, no less—but *someone* has to be practical here.

"Laila, stop." She is no longer amused. I have pushed too far. "I still have some jewelry I can sell, and there are many people who owed your father favors. They will provide, if I ask." She shoos me away like a housefly.

I may be a child in her eyes, but at least *I* know that the favors owed my father died when he did. There will be no one coming to our rescue. "Fine," I say, knowing when to quit. "But you should sell the jewelry soon."

She ignores me, so I join Bastien on the couch. "You shouldn't eat so much of that," I tell him. "You'll get sick again."

He sticks his tongue out at me. "I like it."

I smile at him and mess his hair. He alone seems to be flourishing here. Perhaps I *should* follow his lead.

TRUTHS

I feel shy when I see Emmy next. She knows something about me that I don't know myself. I'd considered slipping away from the dinner table last night to finish the article in secret, but there hadn't been a chance. I spent the meal stuck between Mr. Davis's beetle-browed silence and statements up-talked into chirpy questions by Mrs. Davis. *So I hear you're fitting in well at SCHOOL? It must be so hard to move so FAR AWAY? Emmy has told us so much ABOUT YOU?*

It was a pleasant enough evening, but it has left me feeling stripped bare.

Now I feel a childish need to keep a secret from Emmy, for no other reason than to prove that I can. The opportunity presents itself quickly.

"Want to go to Starbucks with some of us after school?" Emmy asks.

I shake my head. "I have a doctor's appointment," I lie. It

is an unsatisfying fib, though. My dishonesty has no substance, no purpose, and the very moment it comes from my mouth, I realize I have harmed only myself. The realization that I *do* want to go to Starbucks with Emmy makes me irritable. I squash down my churlish mood and add a loophole to my lie. "If it doesn't take too long, maybe I can meet you there after?" My statement-as-question sounds like Emmy's mother.

"Great!" Neither my lie nor my reversal ruffles Emmy. But as I turn to walk away, she stops me. "Laila? Wait a second." She's suddenly nervous, twisting her hair around her fingers. "I'm sorry about last night. My parents, I mean. They're acting really weird lately. Tense, you know?"

"I didn't notice." My answer is the truth—I hadn't sensed anything wrong.

"Okay, good. I'm glad." Emmy gnaws on her lip for a moment before snapping back to the perkier version of herself. "Okay, then. I'll see you later. Try to make it to Starbucks if you can."

I nod, and when school lets out, I look for somewhere I can wait out my fictional appointment. The library seems like my best option. I figure that I can spend an hour there, then join Emmy and her friends with a clean conscience.

My plan dissolves as soon as I enter.

Where I'm from, libraries are like museums. They're rare—locked and guarded vaults that house only books and documents that have long outlived any practical value. Compared to the dusty archives of my past, the room before me seems as garish and industrious as a neon-lit convenience store. The scattered magazines, glowing computer terminals, and overeager literacy posters on the walls first strike me as disrespectful and irreverent. But it doesn't take long before I realize the magic of this library: this is a place that was built to be *used*.

I try to find my way on my own at first, without luck. There are simply too many rows with too many shelves with too many books for me to make sense of. I've never done this type of research before. Back home my tutors supplied me with all the information I needed to write my papers. Compared to my spoon-fed former self, I now feel like an explorer in the thick of a great paper jungle.

I trace my finger along the spines of the books as I wander through the stacks, as if the correct one might send out a signal, or perhaps even leap into my hand. Far from feeling discouraged when no such thing happens, I'm intrigued. There are so many mysteries in these books, so many stories both happier and more tragic than my own, and for a moment I'm tempted to pluck one from the shelf at random just to escape into its pages for an afternoon.

But I can't do that now. I have a new mission; I'm no longer just killing time. I lurk near the librarian's desk for a few minutes, watching. I want to eavesdrop, to learn the right way to ask for help from the white-haired woman who sits there. No one approaches her, though. I have no one to emulate, so I just hover awkwardly.

Before long the woman looks up at me. "Can I help you find something?"

"Yes. I'm trying to find information about—" I falter. I'd almost said *about my father*. I catch myself just in time and give his name instead. I do not claim him as my own, a lie of omission, and his name sounds sterile and impersonal coming from my mouth.

The librarian knows of him. "Hmmm. He died just recently, didn't he? I feel like I saw an article about him earlier this week." She sorts through a stack of magazines, looking for the right one. "Ah. I knew it!" She hands over a magazine turned to a page bearing a photo of my father. "Wait just a minute, dear. I think there might be another article in a magazine in the stacks."

She walks away quickly, energized by the hunt.

I feel a sense of relief, as if I had just gotten away with something. The librarian cared more about the location of the information than the subject matter itself—she would have responded the exact same way had I asked for articles about tractors or kumquats or the history of jazz music. My father's name was nothing but a searchable word, news of his death interchangeable with any current event. I was accustomed to my family name eliciting far more passionate responses. In my experience, people either loved my father or hated him—visceral preferences strongly, even violently, expressed. The librarian's emotionless, businesslike response was disconcerting.

She returns empty-handed. "I can't find the magazine I was thinking of. But you'll have better luck searching online anyway. While you're doing that, I can pull a few books. Do you have a user account?"

I shake my head, scared this will mean that I can't use the computers.

"No problem. I can help you get started." She directs me

over to an empty terminal and guides me through the account setup. If she recognizes the similarity between our research subject and my own name as I enter it she does not say so, and I appreciate her discretion.

When she leaves, my fingers stiffen over the keyboard. *Are you sure you want to do this?* I ask myself. *Are you sure you want to know?* I'm not sure of anything, really. But I do know that certain words have been planted in my head, and they are sprouting like unwelcome weeds:

Dictator. This one compliments of Emmy.

King. A tale told by my mother.

Massacre. An accusation in a newspaper.

Assassination. A sentence carried out by my uncle.

This library—this cluttered room filled with so much information—is the only place where I can sift through the words. I hope that I can disprove them, replace them. *Let them be lies,* I plead silently.

I will my fingers to type.

VISITORS

It's too late to meet Emmy at Starbucks; I'm certain she's long gone. I've been here for hours, held hostage by the pages and pages before me on the endless, unrelenting internet. The librarian, trying to be helpful, also brought me a heavy stack of books detailing my family's history. More information than I ever wanted. More information than I want.

It's too much.

In article after article, my father's name lives on in terrible configurations with terrible events. "Repressive regime," that damning alliteration, chases him throughout the newspapers like a dog nipping at his heels. Protests alternate with massacres; peace talks end with violent deaths. My country makes shameful lists: Worst countries for women. Worst countries for human rights. Worst countries for press freedom. It's never at the top, but it's often close—it's the runner-up in a devil's beauty pageant.

And over and over again, Emmy's word appears. *Dictator.* A title passed down from my grandfather, a man who died before I was born and whose name is similarly tarnished in the pile of books left by the librarian. I stopped reading at my great-grandfather's mention—the pattern was clear by then.

Ours is a cursed dynasty.

The library is closing, and I've learned more than I bargained for. There's nothing to do but go home.

I walk fast, pumping my arms, as if motion could shake the barbed words out of my brain. I've followed this route enough times now to finally know my way, but it's getting dark outside and the changing light makes everything look foreign once again. I spot the familiar chicken-by-the-bucket restaurant, and even that looks ominous now—the long line of cars queued up for the drive-through reminding me of a funeral procession. It's not Colonel Sanders's fault. My library reading has left me with death on the brain.

I'm startled when I walk into our apartment—I almost back out, half convinced I've walked into the wrong unit.

We have company.

The three of us have been alone in our suburban exile for more than a month, so I am momentarily speechless. My mother is not.

"Laila, darling, close the door. Look who's here!" Her voice is brighter and more animated than it has been for weeks. She sounds like her old self.

The man sitting on the couch is vaguely familiar, but I can't remember his name. I should say hello, but I'm fixated on the cup of tea in his hand. I'm certain that I used the last tea bag the day before, so does this mean Mother finally went shopping?

"Laila," she prompts again, sounding impatient.

I nod in greeting.

"Hello, Laila." The man nods back. "I came to check on all of you, to see how you're settling in. I brought a little housewarming present."

A basket sits on the table, bright green cellophane pulled away to reveal fruit and small tins and boxes of food and candy. *That's where the tea came from,* I realize grimly, disappointed that Mother hadn't managed to get it on her own.

I remember the man now. He looks different sitting calmly in our tiny living room, wearing a suit and tie. The last time I saw him was rushed and frantic, and he'd been wearing dirt-stained cargo pants and a holstered gun. "Hurry up! Hurry up!" he'd been yelling at Mother as she tried to pack more and more suitcases. "There's no time for any of that!" His American accent was jarring to me then—an exotic sound in our part of the world, its presence in our home underscoring just how wrong things had gone. He'd driven with us to the airport, looking over his shoulder again and again as he shooed us onto the waiting jet. I hadn't thought of him since. He's a part of a day that is better left unremembered.

Now he looks bland and harmless. Which probably means that he isn't.

An awkward silence settles around us, and the man takes the hint. "I'd better get going," he says, standing up and handing his empty teacup to my mother.

The way she takes the cup in both hands, gracious and smiling as if it were a gift, instantly makes me suspicious. I wonder what I've missed.

"Give it some thought," the man says to my mother. "I'll check back with you later this week."

She *mm-hmm*s noncommittally and walks him to the door. She has always been skilled at not giving answers.

"Where's Bastien?" I ask as soon as she shuts the door.

"I told him to wait in his room while the grown-ups talked." She plucks an orange out of the gift basket and begins to peel it. "Would you like some?" She holds a section of the orange out to me as she calls my brother. "Bastien, my sweet prince, you can come out now!"

It's enough to set me off. "Why do you do that? Why do you insist on calling him that?" I'm suddenly angry with her. Furious, even. I'm hungry, I'm tired, and my head is full of so many questions I don't even know where to begin. I miss my home, my bedroom, my tutor, my things. I miss my father. I miss my life. And now she's the only one left, the only one standing in front of me, so she gets the blame by default. "It's a lie. You know that, don't you? He's no prince. And Father was no king. Can't we stop pretending?" I'm yelling louder than I mean to, and angry tears start to burn at my eyes.

She stares at me for a moment, her eyes narrowed. "You don't know what you're talking about, Laila. Just take some fruit."

I bat the orange away. "I *do* know what I'm talking about. Do *you*?" I stop talking as I see Bastien standing in the doorway of our room. He tilts his head at me but says nothing. I don't know how much he's heard. He doesn't look upset, but then again, he rarely does.

"Can I have some now?" he asks, gesturing toward the basket.

"Of course, darling." Mother shoots a sharp glance in my direction that tells me our conversation is over.

At least we agree on that much.

BEGINNINGS

It's much easier to give someone the silent treatment when you live in a palace—high ceilings and chandeliers have a way of absorbing silences that our little apartment here cannot.

Mother and I stumble over one another in our awkward, wordless state for two days before she gives in. She'd been nervous, jumpy, ever since my blowup, picking at her cuticles and drinking too much coffee while staring off into space. Part of me is proud that I can affect her so much. I could have held out longer.

"Laila, sit." She pats the space on the couch next to her after Bastien goes to bed. "Let's talk."

I sit, but I still don't speak. I want to see where she starts. She'll have a strategy, of course. She always does.

"Laila, there's something that I've never told you. Something about when you were just born."

I'm surprised by her beginning. I don't recognize this strategy.

"Did you know that you were born two months premature?"

I didn't. I shake my head.

She looks at my feet as she speaks, avoiding my eyes. "There were . . . complications. Our hospitals are awful now, and they were even worse back then. But your father thought it would look bad if I flew to London to have a baby, the way your aunts did. The way I did when Bastien was born. Your father thought I should stay at home to make a statement: if the health-care system was good enough for the birth of *his* daughter, then it should be good enough for everyone else."

I fidget, anxious for her to get to the point. I don't want a lecture on health-care policy.

She ignores my impatient sigh. She's determined to tell her story *her* way. "When you came so early, you were tiny. You were so fragile, and so sickly the doctors in that wretched excuse for a hospital didn't think you would even survive. Your father and I were both devastated, but it was worse for him. He blamed himself for putting politics before your health. So he came to the hospital every single day and sat with you. He would just stare at you, stare at all the monitors and tubes keeping you alive, for hours at a time."

She looks me in the eyes only briefly before lowering her gaze once more. "You need to understand, Laila, just how unusual this was for a man in your father's position. He had a country to run, but he came to your side every day."

My mother's voice is tense. I'm alive, so this story should

have a happy ending, but she doesn't sound as if she's telling a happy story.

"*I* was not by your side, though. I refused to even name you." Her eyes fill with tears and her jaw quakes—a sight so rare that I forget to be angry with her. I move closer to her on the couch.

"I couldn't bear it," she continues quickly. "They said you would die, so I couldn't bear to name you, to sit with you. I thought it would just make it worse, make it that much harder when you finally died, if I acknowledged you. In my mind, you were already lost, and the tiny person lying in that incubator was just a ghost there to torment me."

I'm paralyzed on the sofa, too shocked by this confession to react.

Mother takes a deep breath and continues. "Your father *did* name you. He called you Samira. Oh, how we fought over that. I rarely challenged your father about anything, Laila—you know that. But I fought him day and night on that name. For me, it was a betrayal. He was prolonging my suffering. He was naming my grief."

By now, tears are running down her face. I reach over to take her hand, but she shakes her head violently. "Let me finish," she says. "You need to know this about your father. You need to know that for two long months I refused you a name. I refused you a life. But not him. He had faith that you would live—a faith I did not share. He named you, he sang to you, and he watched over you. And when finally, *finally* it began to look as if you would actually survive, I insisted on changing your name."

She wipes roughly at her eyes and pulls her shoulders back. Her voice turns defensive. "*I* named you Laila. I convinced your father that it was a chance to start over. Samira was the name that death knew you by, I told him. But really, it was because Samira was his daughter. Not mine. Your father acknowledged you when I could not, and so I lost the right to call you by that name."

Just when I think that she's finished, as I'm struggling to find the words to respond, she says one more thing.

"Remember this, Laila. No matter what you hear about your father, no matter what happens, remember that he was the one who had faith in you and love for you when no one else did. Not even me." Her voice drops so low that she almost whispers this.

I crawl over the cushion separating us on the couch and burrow into her arms like a young child, allowing her to hug me and cry softly into my hair. I still haven't said a word to her.

When she finally pulls back and lifts her face, my mother looks older than she did just hours earlier. Her beautiful skin seems etched by lines I've never noticed. Her confession has aged her—she gained no relief from telling me her secret. But even as I forgive her for abandoning me so long ago, I wonder why she decided to tell me now.

I think I know. I feel mean-spirited and wicked for my thoughts, but I can't help it. I can't help but think that the only reason she would shield my father with such a damning confession is because my father desperately needs defending. Which means that he is guilty of what I read about, and perhaps even more.

I hug my mother one more time and then slip wordlessly into my bedroom. It doesn't matter that I still haven't spoken to her. One more day of silence—of neither unwanted questions nor unwanted answers—is probably a blessing for us both.

II.

INTRODUCTIONS

There's a boy staring at me.

We're in the courtyard, waiting for the lunch period to end. Everyone devours their food so quickly here, sometimes not even bothering to sit down. They text and study and walk and drive while they eat food that's been processed, portioned, and plastic-wrapped. It's a sterile, cheerless efficiency that makes me yearn for the leisurely meals from my past, each course lasting longer than an entire dinnertime here. Endless cups of hot, sweetened tea are a fading memory, replaced here by fizzy liquids gulped from Styrofoam containers the size of sand pails. I have to force myself to hurry or else find myself self-consciously eating long after everyone else has finished.

I nudge Emmy. "Why is he staring at me?" I've been relying on her more and more. It seems that the deeper I sink into my new life, the more questions I have. For weeks now, she has been my patient guide.

"Oh my god, I can't believe I forgot to tell you!" Her hands fly up to her face. "That's Ian. He's been asking about you. He claims it's for an article he's writing for the school newspaper, but he's so obviously lying." She leans forward as if she's telling a secret, although no one but me is listening. "He's kind of geeky, but in a good way. He's like a cute hipster dork. Not my type, but a lot of girls think he's hot."

I freeze at the mention of a newspaper. "What does he want?"

Emmy laughs at me. "Duh, he thinks you're cute. He wants to meet you. Here, I'll introduce you."

Before I can do anything to stop her, Emmy stands up and waves Ian over. His face reddens slightly when he realizes that he's been caught staring. *Good.* I'm pleased that he feels ashamed. I haven't yet grown comfortable with how boys and girls interact here. There's something crude and carnal about the way they mingle and touch and talk to one another so casually. It makes me nervous.

Sure enough, Ian sits on the bench next to me, sliding closer than I'm used to. I know it doesn't mean anything here, but when his elbow brushes against mine as he leans over to talk to Emmy, I yank my arm and lean away automatically.

He notices. "Sorry," he says, and jumps to his feet. He looks mortified. "Sorry," he repeats.

Good, I think again, not entirely sure why his discomfort pleases me. He's more aware of the space between us than most of the other boys I've encountered here—bucket-fed giants, bigger than most grown men in my country, who jostle me in the hallways or brush against me in doorways without even noticing.

Emmy is gleeful. She introduces us with a teasing note to her voice that doesn't vanish even when I glare daggers at her. "Ian, Laila. Laila, Ian. You two have a lot in common. Or maybe you don't. I really have no idea. Why don't you talk and figure it out?" She leaps off the bench and skips away, turning back just long enough to wink at me.

Now I am the one who is mortified.

Ian rolls his eyes at Emmy's back. "Subtlety is not her strong point," he says.

He shifts from foot to foot. I fidget on the bench. We at least have our awkwardness in common.

He finally speaks. "So, um, I've heard a lot about you. Well, I've heard about you a lot, anyway. I guess that's different, isn't it?"

He's rambling. I let him—perhaps a cruel thing to do, but I don't know the rules here. I feel vulnerable without Emmy to translate his shifting weight, his lopsided smile, and his habit of pushing his hair back out of his eyes more often than necessary.

"I know how hard it is to move to a new country," he's saying.

Now I'm interested. "How do you know?"

"We moved around a lot when I was a kid," he says, looking grateful for the foothold my question gives him. "My family, I mean. Sometimes here in the States, but we also spent a couple of years traveling around South America. A few months in Ecuador, almost a year in Paraguay. All over, really."

"Why?" I don't mean to be abrupt, but this question feels somehow important to me.

"My parents were working as missionaries." He holds his hands up quickly, palms out. "But wait. Don't be freaked out by that. I'm not trying to convert you or proselytize or anything. I'm not like that. At all. They're not either, really. It was just a thing they did."

I keep my face neutral, but in my mind I put up an invisible barrier between us. Newspapers. Religion. Two things that have torn apart my family. Ian has two strikes against him, even if he does seem sweet. "It's nice to meet you," I say, standing up from the bench. I pick up my backpack and start to edge away. I know I'm being rude, and I hope he doesn't take it personally. It's not him. It's what he represents.

Ian, perceptive once again, hears the stiffness in my voice and doesn't try to prolong the conversation. His half wave goodbye shows his confusion, though. "See you around?"

I nod once and he looks encouraged. As I walk away, I realize that I'm smiling. It was purely an accident, that smile, and I hope that Ian didn't see it.

RECOGNITION

More visitors.

This time I come home to a group. Five men, a boy my age, and my mother. They're squeezed three to the couch, and the rest on the rickety seats that usually circle the table where we eat. Mother holds court from the one and only chair in our apartment that doesn't fold up for storage.

This is no social call, I see immediately. There's tension in the air, and everyone except my mother seems edgy and cheerless. She alone looks poised and controlled—she is a woman whose face gives away nothing. She is also accustomed to hosting cheerless gatherings—a souvenir from her old life. She and my father used to plot out her role in advance of important meetings—where to sit, what to say, who to charm and who to snub. She was very good at this.

Even so, she looks relieved to see me. "Laila, there you are. You're late. There's someone here I want you to meet."

Her voice is artificially merry, and I wonder if the others in the room can hear her nervousness, even if they can't see it. Probably not. She hides it well. "Laila, this is Amir. He goes to your school!" She says this as if it were an incredible coincidence worthy of exclamation.

Amir does not move from his chair. He just sits there, still as a statue. Only his eyes give any hint that he has heard my mother's introduction.

His eyes are full of hate.

It's hard to describe what hate looks like, but so easy to spot it. To feel its heat. His eyes are narrowed and locked onto my own—the trajectory of his hatred unmistakable.

I reflexively take a step backward and nearly stumble over Bastien's new backpack, which is lying on the floor. I catch myself just in time to keep from falling, but I still feel off balance.

I don't recognize Amir or any of the other men, but I do recognize their features. They have the burnt-almond eyes, deep olive skin, and high cheekbones of the northwest region of my country. The Trouble Spot, my father used to call it. What little I know about the region, or its people, comes from overheard bits of hushed conversations and brief mentions in my library readings. What little I know all points to these people being enemies. Of my father, at least, which I think means of the rest of my family as well.

And yet my mother now welcomes them into her home.

She pauses a moment, giving Amir a second chance to respond. When he doesn't, she pushes harder. "Laila, won't you please ask Amir to help you in the kitchen? There's a tray of food ready, but it's quite heavy."

I don't often disobey my mother, but this time I do. I take my cue from Amir and remain silent. One of the men snickers, but everyone else is quiet. I feel the weight of their collective scorn—it's not just coming from Amir—and I am nearly overcome with the need to flee.

"Bastien!" I call out. My voice is too loud in the quiet, tense room. "Bastien, are you in there?" I know that he must be. His backpack on the floor and the closed bedroom door are proof. "Come on, I'll take you to the playground."

Now my mother is glaring at me too.

Fortunately, Bastien bursts out of the door almost immediately. He must have been pressing his ear against it, listening. I grab his hand, even though I know he hates it when I do that, and pull him out of the apartment.

"What are they doing here?" I hiss as soon as we're outside. "What do they want?"

Bastien shrugs and then points to someone on the far side of the playground. "*He* told Mother to invite them."

"He" is the man from the other day. The one with the gift basket.

"Go play," I command Bastien, and he runs to the basketball court to watch the older boys practicing jump shots.

The man is leaning against the building, smoking, but he's doing it in a way that makes it obvious he's not a smoker. He's holding the cigarette strangely, like a pencil, and he never lifts it to his mouth to inhale. It burns away, forgotten between his fingers. He's using it as a prop—a reason to linger, I think.

"Hello, Laila." He does not seem surprised to see me.

"I don't know your name," I respond.

"Darren. Darren Gansler." He drops his cigarette to the ground without having taken a single puff that I could see, as if its purpose had already been accomplished. Was he waiting for me?

"You don't look like a Darren." I realize this is ridiculous as soon as it's out of my mouth. I know nothing about what a Darren does or doesn't look like. I do, however, know what a liar looks like. He looks like a liar, this man who has followed us from the worst day of my life to here.

He shrugs. "You're probably right."

He is utterly indifferent to my challenge. He knows that I know he's a liar. But he doesn't care. "What are you doing here?" I ask, even though I suspect he'll just lie to me in response.

"Waiting to talk to your mother," he says, then ducks away to answer the cell phone that begins to ring from his pocket.

Frustrated, I walk off. I'm not going to get any answers from this Darren who isn't Darren anyway, and I'm offended to have been so easily dismissed. But I am certain that neither his presence nor the men in my apartment can possibly mean anything good.

COMPENSATION

The days that follow bring no answers.

Mother is vague about the gathering; my questions only invite pinched lips and irritable head shakes from her. She's suddenly busy all the time—not an easy thing to accomplish in our tiny, distractionless apartment. Bastien didn't overhear anything useful either, so I am left alone with my confusion. At least one surprise comes from the meeting, though.

Food.

I arrive home from school to find the refrigerator and the cabinets full. Mother must have gone to a hair salon too, because the gray streaks that were beginning to snake their way through her hair have vanished. She laughs and waves away my questions. "Just enjoy it, Laila. I bought you something special—look in your bedroom."

I walk into the room expecting to find a small trinket, or maybe a new blouse. Instead, I find a laptop computer sitting on my bed, brand-new and still in its box. It's the same kind as Emmy's, but a more recent version. Bastien's bed has a box on it too—it looks like a video game console of some sort.

I rush back to the living room, positive there's been a mistake. "But these things are so expensive! How did you get them?"

Mother laughs again, then twirls around in the middle of the room. She's wearing a new dress. It looks like it cost as much as my computer, if not more. She's always had expensive taste.

"Mother, where did you get the money for all this?" My heart is pounding in my chest, partly because I'm excited to have my own computer, but more because I'm afraid of what these gifts mean. Did she trade the last of her jewelry for one final splurge, or has she bartered something else? It pains me that I can't just accept, can't just enjoy. But I can't. There's something stopping me, even if it is only the perpetual sourness that seems to run, corrosive and sluggish, through my veins these days.

"I told you that money would come." She is smug. Proud. Standing there, stunning and confident in her expensive new dress and young-again hair, she could be a snapshot from our past—a photo ripped in half, my father's image torn away.

But I'm tired of the way she dances around questions. I have a right to know.

"Mother!" My voice is shrill as I repeat my question. "Where did you get the money for these things?"

Her head snaps up. She's said nothing about my small act of rebellion the day before, but I know there is a tally in her mind. Confronting her, questioning her, is my second act of defiance in two days. She's indignant, but after trying out her anger for just a moment, she softens and discards it. "It's from Mr. Gansler. Darren. I'm doing a little work for him, and in exchange he's going to pay our expenses for a while."

"What kind of work?" My mother has never worked a day in her life, and I find it difficult to imagine what she could be doing that would be worth a laptop, a silk dress, and cupboards stuffed full.

"Just some networking," she says. "I'm making some connections for him. In our community here."

I wasn't aware that we had a community. I certainly haven't felt a part of one. And I know for a fact that my mother would never have allowed me to cross paths with someone like Amir back home, much less introduced us. But I feel relief. This explains why my mother, long accustomed to servants attending her every need, was herself serving tea and cookies to a group of men who looked like they'd never come within miles of someone from her station in life. Her old station, that is.

I fight back the sourness before I respond. Why am I the only one who seems to feel luck like a sunburn? Why should I be the one to question our sudden good fortune? I swallow my questions and resolve to be more like Bastien and my mother. To just accept.

"That's good news," I force myself to say.

Mother relaxes, smoothing the fabric of her skirt as she sits down. She'd been tensed for an argument, ready to do battle with me over this. "Yes, I think that it will be good for all of us. But I'll need your help, Laila, if I'm going to make this work."

I can't imagine how I can possibly help, but she tells me before I ask.

"Amir. I need you to be nicer to him next time. I'm going to be working with his family, so they may be here quite often. There are a lot of them living in this area, and they're well established here. They have connections I need."

"What do you want me to do with Amir, exactly? Seduce him? Marry him?" I say it for shock value, my small way of lashing out, but Mother bats away the provocation.

"I just want you to distract him, Laila. He has a bad attitude, and it would help me if you could keep him entertained while I talk to the adults. He has a way of making unpleasant comments that keep us from moving forward." Her voice turns bladelike. If I am sour, then my mother is sharp. "Kind of like another teenager I know."

What can I say to this? If I am to become someone who attracts, rather than suffers good fortune, then I suppose that I should do its bidding. I swallow my questions yet again and nod.

OPENINGS

"Is it stuck?" Ian slides out of the crowd to lean against the locker next to mine. His shirt has a dime-sized hole on one sleeve, and the bottom of his backpack is stained with blue ink—small flaws I notice only because I'm avoiding eye contact.

"No. I—" I'm flustered, too embarrassed to find a clever lie. "I can't remember the combination. I know it's stupid. I've opened it dozens of times." My brain is spongy lately. Porous. Useless memories seep in, unbidden and unwanted, while necessary facts leak out.

"Close your eyes."

I don't. "What? No."

He smiles and shifts his bag to the other shoulder. "I'm serious, just try it. Close your eyes and try opening the lock. You won't get it exactly right, unless you've got some sort of Jedi Master mind thing going on, but maybe it'll trigger your memory."

I don't disguise my heave of a sigh, but I do close my eyes.

He's right. Blind, the padlock feels more familiar to me. I turn it right, left, right, and then yank. The lock doesn't yield, but something in my mind does and I remember that the first number is fifteen. I open my eyes and the next two numbers stumble back to me as well.

"Thank you." I face my open locker, but he's still in the corner of my vision.

"No worries. I forget my combination every time we have more than a three-day weekend. But the muscle memory is always there. Your hands remember things even when your brain doesn't. At least, that's my official, scientific explanation." He grins and pushes away from the locker. "See you around?"

I turn toward him at last and nod. His eyes are an unusually pale shade of hazel and they give him an intense, almost leonine appearance. "Yes."

I wait until he leaves before I look down at my hands. *Muscle memory.* I've never heard that term before, but it makes sense. I've been trying to will away the unwelcome thoughts of my last days at home, but my body can't be denied the things that trigger. Familiar smells and sounds, a blast of hot air from a passing bus, even the sight of a bottle of water the same brand that someone—I don't even know who—thrust into my hands as I sobbed and retched through the plane's takeoff. . . .

I shut the locker and hug my books against my chest as I walk to class, trying not to brush against anyone or even breathe too deeply, lest some lingering odor attack my senses with false familiarity. If I can't control my memories, then perhaps I can at least escape the triggers.

AIR

I've been underwater for nearly a month.

That's what it feels like here—a life submerged. Wave-tossed and sand-scoured. Voices around me in school sound muted and distorted; faces are out of focus. I'm experiencing my new life through fathoms of water, making everything seem dreamlike and unreal, as if my brain can only accept so much change before it drowns.

Gradually, though, I've been surfacing. Certain things, certain people, have been pulling me out of my floating state, whether I like it or not.

Emmy, for example. After all this time—these weeks that have felt like years—she is still here, still hasn't discarded me in favor of a new specimen for her rotating collection of friends. And she does not take no for an answer.

"I knew you'd say no. But it's just a dance, and I already

have the perfect dress for you to wear. It's too small for me now, but it would definitely fit you. You're so tiny!"

From her this is a high compliment. She and her friends are fiercely competitive in their suffering to be smaller, and even now Emmy is peeling the cheese and pepperoni off a slice of pizza—she's gone vegan this week. Around the lunch table everyone seems to have given something up—dairy, meat, gluten, sugar, carbs. Only in a land of plenty could people voluntarily go without so much.

"Laila, you *have* to! You'll have a great time, I swear!" Emmy lives her life in exclamation marks. Tori and Morgan, her sometimes-friends, nod in agreement.

I shake my head and try not to smile. They'll take it as a weakness and keep pushing. We've formed an unlikely group lately, based, I suspect, on my novelty and Emmy's cheerful efforts. There's an undercurrent of tension between the others, the remnants of a nebulous summertime feud. Something involving name-calling, recanted party invitations, and other such suburban tragedies, according to Emmy's version of events. Teenage betrayals, largely forgiven but certainly not forgotten. I seem to relieve the tension somehow; my newness and my foreignness give them an outlet, and together they fuss over me.

"Quit bugging her. She can decide whether she wants to come or not." Morgan alone is skeptical of me, which I think makes her the smartest one of the bunch. Emmy's unwavering determination to be my friend still makes me nervous, though I find myself letting my guard slip around her more and more.

"I can't," I tell them. "I would be so uncomfortable.

Things like that don't exist where I'm from. It would never be allowed."

"But you're here now. New place, new rules. Aren't you even curious?" Emmy has already made up her mind that I will go to the homecoming dance. "Besides"—a sly look crosses her face—"Ian asked me if you'd be there."

"Ooooo," Morgan and Tori chorus, teasing me.

I have not needed their help to decipher Ian's attention lately—some things are universal. To his credit, he has kept a respectful distance. But he hovers on the edge of my days, and I see him watching me. I sometimes watch him back.

"So?" Tori asks. She's the one I know the least about—her pale blondness for some reason makes her forgettable to me. "Will you come with us?"

I could say that my mother won't allow it. In another lifetime, she wouldn't have. But here, she is newly permissive—liberated by the distance from the rules of our past, perhaps. Or, more likely, just distracted by the burdens of the present. Here, she will tell me to go.

Finally, I nod. I *am* curious.

RESOLVE

I don't know why I agreed to go. All day the decision haunts me, and I sit through my afternoon classes in even more of a fog than usual. The teachers don't notice. I'm one more foreign student in a district teeming with the children of immigrants, lesser embassy staff, and expat employees of budget-strapped NGOs who can't afford the rent closer in to the city. We are transient students with heavy accents who show up one term and vanish the next. We are invisible in class.

"Can anyone comment on the particular importance of the first ten amendments to the Constitution?" The teacher's eyes skim over those of us in the classroom who can speak most personally about the absence of such rights. I do not raise my hand, nor do the two other students in the room who come from elsewhere. I know very little about them—rather than bonding over our shared experiences, we repel one another, as though afraid our foreignness might metastasize if we get too close.

Only one student volunteers; she traces the words with her index finger as she reads from her textbook. "The Bill of Rights establishes fundamental personal freedoms and limits the role of central government."

I'm angry with myself for being nervous about the prospect of an American dance. Such a silly, petty concern. But I don't know how to act. I don't know how to dance, at least not in the way television shows me it's done here.

I *do* have a fluttery thrill at the thought of doing something that would horrify my uncle, though. He once slapped my mother hard enough to make her mouth bleed for allowing me to swim in a bathing suit while there were male visitors at the house. He tried to hit me, too, but she stepped between us and absorbed the second blow—the one meant for me. She spit a bloody spray at his feet and dragged me away, telling me to ignore him even as he hissed ugly threats at her. I waited for her to tell my father that evening, but she never did. "Your father has bigger problems to address with his brother than a little quarrel about clothing," she'd explained.

Almost as if she had predicted what would happen.

The memory strengthens my resolve. I will go. I will dance.

"Come on, class. No one has any thoughts on this? Really?" The irritation in Mrs. Moore's voice draws my attention back to the moment. She looks at the clock on the wall and sighs. "We're all stuck with this topic for the next fifteen minutes, so someone might as well answer. Let's try the question another way: Why do we even have amendments?" She looks hopefully at the front row, but no one responds.

"Is it because the Founding Fathers made so many mistakes? Is the Constitution just so screwed up that we have to keep going in to fix it?" She switches tactics: mild sarcasm now—American civics–style.

"Yeah. They did screw up." Someone in the third row finally speaks. "Especially the part where they tried to ban alcohol. *That* was stupid." He grins and twirls his pen around his fingers until someone from the other side of the room shouts back.

"That wasn't the Founding Fathers, dumbass. That *was* one of the amendments."

Both comments draw laughs, and the teacher looks ready to give up.

"It's just . . . change."

Mrs. Moore's eyebrows go up when I speak, and then she nods. "Okay, let's talk about that a little more. What kind of change? Are people so different now than they were back in 1787 that we need completely different laws?" She gestures for me to answer.

I don't want to, but now everyone is staring. "No, n-not exactly," I stammer. "It's more an issue of—" My vocabulary fails me under the weight of the attention. "Context."

But the teacher won't let me stop there. "Continue," she says.

I fray the edges of my blank notebook while I speak. "I don't think it's that *people* have changed so much. I mean, they have, obviously. But sometimes it's more that things around us change so much that something that might have seemed unimaginable all of a sudden feels . . . inevitable."

"In-ev-i-ta-ble." I hear someone imitate my voice, high-pitched and haughty, and I wish I hadn't said anything at all.

"Well put," Mrs. Moore says, which makes it even worse. I feel my face flush and I clutch unconsciously at the veil I no longer wear, then sink deep into my seat until the bell rings.

But even as I hurry out, regretting the loss of my classroom invisibility, my mouth forms the liberating word again: *context*. This new world of mine is neither my *then* nor my *there*. If I am to be forced to live in exile from my past, I might as well take advantage of the freedoms my new context offers.

I might as well dance.

OBLIGATIONS

Before homecoming comes another, less celebratory type of dance.

I take the long way home most days, shuffling more than walking. I've been learning new streets—every block that becomes familiar expands my world by a fraction. Already I feel more comfortable walking alone here; the space and the freedom are no longer intimidating. My circuitous routes also give me a reason to come home later and later.

Today I should be hurrying, but I'm not. Today Amir and his cousins will be at our apartment. I'm expected to chip through his hatred and make him my friend—a task that feels impossible.

I've already decided that I will make only the smallest effort, just enough to appease my mother without actually succeeding, when I see Mr. Gansler once again leaning against our building.

"Laila." He calls me over. He's not bothering with the cigarette this time.

I consider ignoring him, but it seems pointless. I have a feeling that "Darren Gansler," true name unknown, will follow me with his bad luck wherever I go.

"I guess I shouldn't be surprised to see you here today."

He raises an eyebrow and studies me for a moment before speaking. "You strike me as an intelligent young woman, Laila. So I probably don't have to tell you just how important these meetings are for your family."

There's a question hiding behind his statement. He wants to find out how much I know. The answer, of course, is not much at all, but I don't want him to realize that.

His mouth pinches up on one side—not quite a smile—and he crosses his arms over his chest. He's guessed.

"It looks like I *do* have to tell you." He says it in a way that sounds like he wishes he didn't, and his smirk wilts into a frown. "Laila, I didn't bring your family here out of the goodness of my heart. You're here, or at least your mother is here, for a reason. Your mother made a deal the day you all got on the plane. We—the United States government, that is—went to considerable risk to get your family out of your country safely. I offered your mother a way out and guaranteed political refugee status here if she agreed to cooperate."

I know exactly what he is going to say next before it even comes out of his mouth.

"Her cooperation hasn't been exactly . . . perfect."

I have to bite the inside of my cheek to keep from laughing out loud. That my mother would not do his bidding should surprise no one. *You are more conniving than the devil himself, dearest Yasmin,* my father used to tell her. *You are truly my secret weapon.* His words were always delivered with a kiss—he admired her cunning.

Mr. Gansler does not.

"As I said, Laila, you seem like an intelligent girl." He speaks quietly, as if he doesn't want anyone to overhear. "So I'm sure you understand just how important it is that your family remain here in the U.S. Obviously I can't guarantee your safety if you go back home. No one can. I'd hate to see that happen."

I manage to keep my expression neutral, but I can't breathe. The threat is clear. Do what he wants, or he'll send us back. We all know that can't happen. It just can't.

Slowly, my breath returns, but I can still hear my heart thudding in my ears like a war drum. I study him before responding—this bland, ill-pressed-trouser-wearing man. His expression is mild and open, almost friendly. As if he'd just asked me about the weather, or how I liked school.

I hate him, if only for his proximity to our suffering.

I pull my shoulders back and stand as tall as I can, wishing that for once I could tower over someone. I make no effort to conceal my disgust. "Whatever agreement my mother made, she made it on the day she watched my father die. You were there. You heard the mob chanting outside the gates. What *wouldn't* she have agreed to? What choice did she have?"

Mr. Gansler doesn't answer. He has said enough, and he sees that I understand him. He offers only a small apologetic nod and then walks away.

I'm motionless as I watch him leave, afraid to test my wobbly, weak knees. I don't know exactly what my mother agreed to, but for now it doesn't matter. I saw in his eyes that he means to carry out the threat. Mr. Gansler has transferred the burden of her agreement to me, and I have no choice but to comply.

FRIENDSHIP

I'm rattled by the encounter. So rattled that I don't notice Amir sitting on my doorstep until I almost trip over him. I curse my luck—today seems to be the day for surprise encounters with unwelcome men.

"Do you want to come inside?" I don't know why he's alone out here, but my mother would be furious if I didn't at least invite him in.

"I'm not exactly welcome in there." He's angry, sulking.

A small surge of hope rises in my chest. Had I been relieved of my duty? "Did my mother say that?"

He makes a snorting sound. "Your mother has a way of making herself perfectly clear without saying anything at all."

I can't help but smile at that.

"She told me she was worried that you were so late and asked me to go out and find you."

"So you just sat down out here?" It shouldn't matter, but

I feel offended. That he hasn't even bothered to stand up to speak with me doubles the insult.

His jaw muscles clench. "No. Actually I did exactly as I was told. I went out to find you, but I didn't get far before I saw that you were busy talking to someone else." He tilts his head to the side and his tone turns challenging. "Is he a friend of yours?"

I break eye contact with him. I don't want to answer this question. I don't know what the answer should be. Darren Gansler is certainly no friend, but for some reason I don't want Amir to know that. I know how poorly-chosen alliances can end. Finally, I shrug. Let him decipher this nonanswer however he wants.

"You know who he is, right?" Amir won't drop it.

"Does it matter?" Another nonanswer. I want to keep him talking.

"He's CIA. If he's talking to you, it's only because he thinks you're a weak link. That you'll give him something the rest of us refuse to."

Another insult. I rein in my anger. I still need answers. "How do you know?"

He makes that humorless laugh sound again, too joyless and dry for someone his age. My age. "We've had a few go-rounds with him. They didn't end well. Now he gets other people to do his dirty work." He jerks his head toward my door. Toward my family.

My mouth is opening, I'm ready to lash out, when it suddenly occurs to me that we're speaking my language. The sound of home. I'd slipped into it without even noticing, drawn in by the comfort of its familiarity. Although Amir's coarse accent is a strong reminder that he comes from the mountainous border region, it's the first time in weeks that I've heard my language from anyone other than Bastien or my mother. And even Bastien is always speaking in English now—his accent sounding more American every day.

I switch back to English. It makes me feel less vulnerable. "I never see you at school," I say, changing the subject. "Do you really even go there?"

He tenses at the new sound. Boys from his region don't study English with private tutors. Boys from his region often don't go to school at all. From his reaction I can tell that my English is better than his, even though he's surely lived here for longer than I have. *Good,* I think. *Let him be the vulnerable one.*

"I've seen *you.*" His answer, in English, is even more heavily accented than I thought it would be. "You certainly make friends quickly." Even through the language barrier, his words sound like an accusation, although it's one I don't understand.

"You mean Emmy?" It bothers me that he's seen me at school while I haven't seen him. It makes me feel watched. Exposed. "Yes, I suppose I do make friends quickly. With the right people, at least. Unlike you, she's been nothing but kind." I find that I mean the words as I say them. As hard as I've tried to find faults in her attention, Emmy *has* been nothing but kind.

His face twists into a smirk, and I know he's about to say something cruel.

He doesn't have a chance, though. The door bursts open

and the men—Amir's relatives, I assume—stomp out in a flood of indignant words. "Let's go," one of them says roughly to Amir, who jumps to his feet immediately. "She's wasting our time in there."

Amir follows the muttering wave of angry men to the stairwell, then pauses to turn back. "Just be careful around people who try too hard to be your friend here. They may have harmful intentions."

There is no concern in his voice. His words sound more like a threat than a well-meant warning.

I dismiss him like a servant with a flick of my wrist—a gesture that causes the hate in his eyes to flare again before he spins around and follows the men.

He's long gone before it occurs to me that he may not have been talking about Emmy. Did he instead mean Mr. Gansler, with his overstuffed gift baskets and conditional paychecks? I feel foolish for missing the reference, and I suddenly hope that Amir returns soon.

He may hate me, but he also knows something. I'm willing to suffer his scorn in exchange for answers.

TRANSFORMATION

I feel ridiculous.

Emmy, Morgan, and Tori have dressed me up as one of them. I am an American package. Or perhaps I should say a packaged American—an imitation of something wholesome, like processed cheese, another food Bastien has come to adore here.

They don't notice that I'm distracted as they fluff and paint and wrap me. But I am. I can't focus on their debates about my hair—up or down?—or my shoe choice, or even their gentle teasing about Ian, who they've chosen for me as firmly as they've decided upon my dress. My very, very short dress.

It occurs to me to object to the dress, but I don't. I have a hard time caring about the exposure of a few inches of my thighs when my mind is focused on whether or not Mr. Gansler will soon be putting my family on an airplane for the second time.

The rapid, angry departure of the men from our apartment had not disturbed my mother at all. No matter how I pleaded with her to call them, visit them, to make whatever was wrong right again, she just shushed me or patted my head like a child. "Everything is fine, Laila," she'd said in her infuriatingly vague way. "Everyone appreciates what they struggle for more than what they are given. Trust me."

Trust is something I'm finding in short supply, though.

"Trust me, you look *amazing*!" Emmy, too, wants my faith.

"You really do, Laila," Tori echoes. "You look good in red."

Morgan scavenges through Emmy's jewelry box, still unsatisfied with the details of my transformation. "Don't you have any other earrings, Emmy?" She pulls out a pair she finds suitable and holds them up, triumphant, before Emmy can answer. "Perfect!" They're costume pieces, garish and cheap; the painted metal is already peeling.

Still, I don't argue, and when she hands them to me, I put them on dutifully. I might as well—the disguise my friends have chosen for me is a small price to pay for this excursion into American life. Without meaning to, I have grown excited about the evening. The shiny, lipsticked chaos in Emmy's dress-strewn bedroom breaks through my worries in short, welcome bursts. I accept Tori's offer of a spritz of perfume and will myself into the moment.

Morgan fastens the earrings and nods, finally satisfied. "There. You're like our Cinderella for the evening."

Tori giggles. "What does that make us? The mice who sew her dress?"

"No, dummy." Morgan pulls playfully at one of Tori's errant curls. "We're her fairy godmothers." Her expression turns serious—concerned, even. "Do you know the story? 'Cinderella'?"

Emmy steps in to defend me once again. "She's not an idiot, Morgan. Of course she does."

I am amused by their banter. That their passions run so high about everything from salad dressing to fairy tales is endearing. "I think that everyone in the world knows at least the Disney version." I hesitate, not sure if I should continue. But why not share my culture with them, the way they share theirs with me? "My country also has a children's story about a lost slipper, but it has a very different ending."

"Oh, tell us!" Emmy, of course, is thrilled to collect another piece of international trivia. Even Tori and Morgan seem interested, so I go on.

I start slowly, using an exaggerated storyteller's cadence—it's been years since I last heard the tale, and I want to do it justice. I'm embarrassed to find that I feel vaguely competitive, as if my story needs to somehow beat their Cinderella story. "Well, according to our version, there was once a rich and powerful sultan who had a daughter whose beauty was unsurpassed. He favored her above all his other children, and worried constantly that one of his rivals would someday hear of her great beauty and steal her away. To prevent that from happening, the sultan locked her up in a tower filled with many luxuries and servants so that no one from the outside would ever see her face.

"But one day the daughter was standing next to an open

window when she heard the sound of music being played nearby. It was more haunting and beautiful than anything she had ever heard or even dreamed of. Enchanted by the melody, she vowed to do whatever it took to meet the person capable of creating such incredible music.

"She quickly tied together several lengths of the silken curtains draping her windows, climbed to the ground below, and ran as fast as she could in the direction of the sounds. She was so focused on the music in the distance that she didn't even notice when one of her gold-embroidered slippers fell off as she climbed down from her tower. She soon caught up to the musician, a poor but talented traveler, and he fell in love with her upon first sight. They ran away together and were married in secret that very night.

"The sultan was outraged when he heard what had happened, not only because of the loss of his precious daughter, but even more so because of the loss of his honor. He ordered his men to scour the land for his missing daughter. She had anticipated this, however, and so she had already traded her silken robes for the coarse clothing of a peasant and disguised her face behind a veil.

"When the sultan's men failed to find her, he gave them new orders: to go from village to village with the single gold-threaded slipper and try it on the foot of every woman. Whoever's foot fit the slipper was to be killed on the spot."

I barely pause to take a breath. I've found my rhythm in the tale. "Now, unlike in *your* Cinderella story, a shoe size is not such a terribly unique thing, and many innocent women were killed. When the sultan's daughter heard of this, she could not bear to let the deaths continue, and she turned herself in to her father's men at once. The sultan refused to see her. From his private chambers he ordered that she be publicly stoned to death that evening at sunset.

"The musician was despondent. He vowed to play his beautiful bride one last song before her death, even if it meant that he, too, would be sentenced to die. As she was led out to the courtyard where stonings took place, he began to play more sweetly and sadly than he ever had before.

"The sultan, who had been watching from a window, heard the music and softened. No one who could create such enchanting sounds could possibly be dishonorable, he realized. He ordered that his daughter's execution be stopped immediately. His entire kingdom was shocked when he not only forgave the couple but also allowed them to live as man and wife within his palace. In exchange he required only that all of his daughter's toes be cut off so that she could never again run away, and also so that he would never again be offended by the sight of a slipper the size of the one that represented his daughter's shameful act."

I stop abruptly at the end. I'd been so focused on translating the story into English—I was trying hard to capture the subtle nuances that come through in my language—that I hadn't noticed my friends' reactions.

Morgan's upper lip is drawn up in an unmistakable look of disgust. "God, Laila. That's completely . . . *barbaric*. They really tell that story to children?"

Tori is also horrified. "I would've had nightmares for months if I heard that when I was a kid." She shakes her head slowly.

Not even Emmy jumps to my defense this time. Her eyes are wide, and she stays silent.

Barbaric. The word is a slap to my face, the sting worse for the surprise of it. I'm shocked by their shock. I'd never thought of the story as anything but a harmless fable. My own nanny used to embellish the details, describing at length the impossible riches inside the tower, the seductive power of the music, and the details of the father's fury. Sometimes the daughter's entire feet were cut off—my nanny's version didn't always stop at the toes. To me, it was simply a story with a message: family honor, redemption, and true love. Even the sultan was no villain, since in my world a father's love can be measured by the lengths he will go to to protect his daughter, no matter the consequence.

Now, sitting here with my shoulders bared by my borrowed dress and my ears bejeweled with gaudy tin, I hear the other messages in the story for the first time. That I'd actually considered the ending a happy one suddenly strikes me as . . . barbaric.

"Oh my god, you guys, look what time it is. We need to hurry up." This is the most Emmy can do for me, and I flash her a weak smile to let her know I appreciate it.

I am too stunned by the weight of my dark new understanding to hurry. I'm the last out the door, and I leave without so much as a glance in the mirror. I don't need to see my transformation. I can feel it.

CONTEXT

Mrs. Davis takes dozens of pictures in front of the living room fireplace, then volunteers Emmy's dad to drive us to the dance. "It's too far to walk in those shoes, girls; you'll break your ankles. Besides, it's getting dark."

Emmy grabs the camera out of her hands. "Did you get a good one?" We look over her shoulder as she scrolls through the images, grunting her disapproval as she presses buttons. Tori's eyes are closed in this one; Morgan's mouth is open in that one. In photo after photo, Emmy's hair is wrong, she looks too fat, there's too much flash. . . . Her face starts to fall until finally she finds a picture worthy of her collection. "We look so hot!" she crows as we study ourselves in the tiny screen. "Mom, can you print this one, please?"

I stare at my image, pleased and appalled. I am nearly unrecognizable—a bedazzled version of myself held together with spaghetti straps and mounted atop small, spindly heels.

My makeup is too heavy and my hair is too fussy, but somehow it's okay, because . . . I fit. I am one of four satin-clad girls playing dress-up. Back home we'd be lumped in with prostitutes looking like this—the clothing alone would condemn us. Here, though, the innocence of the moment glows through the layers of gloss, and we look like nothing more than happy, pretty girls.

The moment doesn't last. "All right, Cinderellas," Emmy's mom calls as she shoos us out the door. "Your coach awaits you!"

"Mom!" Emmy hisses at her to be quiet, but the Cinderella reference lingers.

"*Awk*-ward," Morgan sings under her breath.

Barbaric, I sing in my head. Group photo aside, their fairy tale is not mine, and we are once again divided.

In the car I choose the passenger seat to accommodate my silence; Mr. Davis doesn't notice, or doesn't care. *Let the others whisper about me in the backseat. Let my face burn until it's surely as shiny and scarlet as my dress.*

One more story from home enters my thoughts as we drive.

Another car, driven by another man. We were always going somewhere, it seems—why else so many memories in transit? I'm wearing another party dress, this one chosen by my mother. Was it pink? Maybe lavender. Something girlish and sweet; I couldn't have been much older than Bastien is now.

I'd started the evening feeling like a princess, but by then I was tired and cranky. Mother shushes me and drapes one of her necklaces over my head to distract me. But neither the icy-sharp feel of the gems nor the satisfying heft of the golden links—all quite real, of course—cheers me. I'd seen enough jewels that evening, thank you very much. My cousin had been insufferable, showing them off.

"How many more of these do we have to sit through?" I complain. "I wish she would just get married and be done with it. How many parties can one bride possibly have?" My voice turns nasal and wicked as I imitate. "*Looook. This one is from my fiancé. And these are from his parents. And this one, and this one, and this one . . .*" I stroke my ears and neck with exaggerated sweeps—a diva displaying her imaginary jewelry.

"Don't envy your cousin, Laila," Mother says into her compact as she wipes lipstick from her teeth. Believing her comment to be a rebuke, I turn toward the window to pout. But she's not done speaking.

"The better the jewelry, the worse the man," she says as she puts away the mirror. She sounds tired, and maybe even a little bit angry, though I can't understand why. She was the one who dragged me to this party, yet another of the endless engagement festivities for my cousin Farah.

"What do you mean by that?" Now I'm indignant. Has she just insulted my father? "*You* have very nice jewelry."

She sighs and fingers the largest of the stones circling my undeserving neck. "Yes, I do. But I chose well. Not everyone gets a choice. Certainly not poor Farah."

The hint of gossip is tantalizing. I scrabble across the leather seat to take Mother's hand and snuggle up against her, shameless in my thirst for unkind stories about my unkind cousin.

For once Mother is reluctant to play along. She plucks the

necklace off me and takes her time refastening it around her own neck. Finally, she speaks. "I shouldn't tell you any of this. But that girl is too young and too stupid to be practically sold off to a miserable old wretch like her husband-to-be. Hers will not be a happy marriage. Not that she'd know one if she saw one, anyway. Not with parents like hers." Mother leans back with her eyes closed and refuses to say anything else on the matter.

I already knew that Farah's marriage had been arranged—something gradually becoming less common, at least in our circles. But my cousin had claimed to be pleased with the match. I knew nothing of the man, except that my uncle had chosen him. That was reason enough to dislike him, though.

"You are worth more than shiny stones, Laila," Mother had whispered as she kissed me good night once we reached home. "We all are." I'd been charmed by the rare display of affection, and I hadn't sought any additional meaning from the words.

Here, in the front seat of Emmy's father's car, I remember them. I also remember the feel of real jewels, so different from the costume version I wear now. I remember the weight of the gold, the strength of the clasps, and the almost-scratches left behind by sharp diamond facets.

I flick irritably at the cheap baubles hanging from my ears, missing the gems of Before. And then I remember one more detail.

Farah had been just sixteen years old.

One year older than I am now, married off to a man more than twice her age. Had I even seen her since? Was she as unhappy as Mother had predicted? I can't recall.

I shiver and try not to think of her any longer. I am *here* now.

MOVEMENT

The heavy, thumping music makes the air in the gymnasium vibrate. For a moment the guttural combination of drumbeats and bass turns familiar, the sound of a procession of tanks driving by, and my heart starts to race. But then the lyrics begin— silly, repetitive lines heavy with rhymes about feeling the night. We are not in a war zone, I remind myself. We are at a school dance. *All right, all right. Feel the night.* My pulse slows and my lungs allow me a breath.

"Laila, come on!" Emmy yells over the music and waves me in, pulling me by the fingertips through a churning mob of dancing bodies. I'm bumped, then jarred, and I lose Emmy, but she reaches back and finds me again. Everyone around me is huge, all sharp elbows and heavy feet, and I feel like I'm being crushed. I'm underwater again, not breathing, until we break through the frenzy to a corner of painted linoleum calm.

"Are you okay?" Emmy is laughing, but she looks concerned.

I nod, not yet trusting my voice. In this life I have only seen such things in an entirely different context. In my experience, such frenzied swarmings mean only riots, and riots mean bloodshed.

"As you can see, there's no requirement that you actually know *how* to dance here. What a bunch of flailing idiots!" Emmy somehow spots Morgan in the chaos and waves her over.

She's pushing her way through when the air-pounding song ends and a new one begins. The crowd reacts by slowing, then dispersing. The sweaty dancers look wilted, dejected by the calmer tempo, and they shuffle and spread to the perimeter of the room.

Morgan rolls her eyes at the deflating scene as she joins us. "Laila, you're shaking!" She places her hand on my shoulder. "What's wrong?"

"I'm just cold." It's a ridiculous thing to say in the swampy heat of the body-packed gym, but my friends accept my answer.

"All the more reason to get out and dance!" Morgan half pushes me toward the center of the room, but I resist. More than anything I just want to leave this noisy, crushing place.

"Laila?" I see in Emmy's face that she will not enjoy the night if I am unhappy. For her, I decide to pretend. I follow Morgan, my feet heavy with dread.

Fortunately, the dance floor is less crowded than when we first entered, and almost all the dancers left are girls. But just as my little group finds a space and we form a small dancing circle of our own, the music changes again. To my ears, the song is hardly different from the one that cleared the space, but the crowd hears something that I cannot. People surge back to the floor, and once again I am being pummeled and suffocated. It takes me several long, breathless moments to realize that it's my frozen stance that's making me suffer—my rigid shoulders and planted feet. I need to stop resisting, I tell myself. I need to move *with* the crowd.

The motion helps. I'm awkward at first; my hips and knees refuse to sway. But Emmy was right—there is nothing to *know* about this kind of dancing. It is simply something to do.

I watch my feet until they seem to be cooperating. It's only when I feel confident enough about my movement that I look up and see what has happened.

Decency has fled the room.

All around me couples writhe and grind against each other in time to the music. It's lewd, animal, and I can't help but freeze in place once more. Next to me, Emmy, sweet Emmy, who even now wears tiny butterfly earrings more suitable for a child, is leaning backward, her arms reaching up and behind her to embrace the boy who is pressed against her like a sweating, grunting human cape. The transformation in the room is complete.

But television has taught me well. I regain my balance quickly, the initial shock worn off. I've seen this, just never in person. In my country, this scene—this lusty, teenage carnival—would end in a police raid and lashings. Or worse. My uncle would be involved. Where judgment could be found, he always was.

That thought—the mere idea of my uncle's reaction—unleashes me. *I'm here in disguise. I can be someone else. Someone other than me.* I am here to learn.

I grant myself a small gift—a moment away from my past.

Loose-limbed, freed, I intentionally bump against the nearest person, a sandy-haired boy I've never seen before. The bump is enough. He turns around, no introductions necessary, and presses against me as if our torsos were magnetized. Behind him, his previous dance partner makes an angry face and then moves on, disappearing into the waves of dancers. I barely register her scorn—I'm trying to stay on my feet as this broad, untucked-shirt-wearing body leans and thrusts against me.

Tori, grinning and grappling with her own partner to my left, sees me and gives me a thumbs-up. "Daaammn, Laila," she says approvingly. Her lipstick is smeared, and her eyes are too bright even in the strobe-lit darkness. It's all surreal.

But that is precisely why I stay. *Because* it's not real.

I don't think. I just do. I press back against my stranger—my partner—and watch my hands find his chest. I push a little, he pushes a little, and since neither of us yields, we're crushed together even closer.

I've been sheltered, even captive, judging from the standards grinding around me, but in my American disguise I find it easy to catch on. I feel out-of-body as I look up at him in a way that I mean to be encouraging, and I link one leg over his so that I'm nearly straddling my stranger's thigh. My dress rides up even higher, and for a second my hand reaches to pull it down, until I remember my purpose. I let the skirt drift where it may.

There are hands on my skin where fabric once lay, and nearby someone howls like a wolf. It was surely done in jest, but the sound is so fitting that it sends chills down my spine. I move my hands. I move my hips. I move my body against his. Never before have I moved like this. I'm surprised to find that I like it, that my ragged breaths are coming and going in time with the breaths of the boy who is touching me— every time we inhale, our chests are pressed together even that much closer. It's not pleasure that I feel, exactly. It's too clinical for that.

It's power.

I've always been taught that women should be invisible, that our bodies must be hidden and our voices hushed. In this moment, with this unknown person grinding against me, I almost understand why. Just looking at the stranger's eyes, heavy-lidded and incoherent, and his hands, gripping and petting as if he were having a stroke, I think: *I have done this.*

It's intoxicating.

I want to test my power further. I'm tilting my head up toward his, my eyes daring him and my mouth slightly open, breathless in a whole new way, when someone grabs my arm and whirls me around roughly. I turn with a smile on my face, eager to discover my next conquest.

It's no dance partner, though. It's Amir.

My spell is broken, and my stranger melts back into the crowd with a shrug. I was just a body; he'll find another. Amir doesn't let go of my arm, so I step closer to him, still moving with the music. I want to dance more. Amir will do.

"Stop it!" he hisses. "You're acting disgusting." He pulls

me toward the exit, moving so fast that I stumble and almost fall. As I catch myself, yanking my arm out of Amir's grip, I see Ian looking at me from a few feet away.

Are you okay? he mouths, since the music is too loud to talk.

I look back at Amir, whose face is twisted and tense with anger. For a second I hesitate, but then I nod at Ian. *I'm fine,* I mouth back to him. After all, Amir is nothing but a displaced peasant—his rage is no threat to me. But I haven't forgotten Mr. Gansler's threat. I need to appease Amir for my family's sake. I will allow him his anger as a peace offering.

Ian's face stays neutral, but he keeps watching until I let the gymnasium doors slam behind me. I'm still charged from the dancing, emboldened by the music I can still hear pounding against the doors and windows. I turn to Amir and smile. Let him rage. *I* am in control.

STEPS

"What the hell were you doing in there?" Amir's voice is a controlled shout close to my ear, so quiet that the smokers leaning against a car in the parking lot barely look up. He is skilled at not drawing attention to himself. "Are you *trying* to shame your family?"

"New place, new rules." Emmy's phrase doesn't sound as tidy in my native tongue, but the meaning is still clear. "I'm just fitting in," I say more gently. I can't forget that I need him. "What are *you* doing here?"

Amir's face flushes, and he looks away. He's *embarrassed*.

I laugh. "I think that maybe you came for the same reason I did? Just to see for yourself?"

He scowls, but it's an embarrassed scowl, and there's humor twitching underneath. He kicks at a cigarette butt on the ground and hides his smile. He also tries to hide his small peeks at me. This sparkly, satin version of me is new to him, too.

I need to encourage this. To make Amir my ally—in curiosity, if in nothing else. "It's certainly different here, isn't it?" I keep my voice light, teasing. "Can you imagine that happening back home?"

Finally, he's willing to show me his smile. It's crooked—interrupted by a scar that traces from his sharp cheekbone down to the corner of his mouth. It's not unattractive. *He's* not unattractive, I realize.

Focus, Laila.

"The people here are children," he says. "All of them. Even the grown-ups."

I wonder how many people not from his own country he has actually spoken to since moving here. "They're not so bad," I say.

"Yeah, I could see in there that you think quite highly of them. One of them in particular."

He's still trying to shame me, but I don't react. I have been shamed by men far more powerful than Amir. Besides, why *should* I feel shame? It wasn't me in there. I was just acting a part, trying on someone else's skin.

"Do you want to sit down?" I nod toward a graffiti-scarred bench close by. "It's a beautiful night."

Amir tilts his head and squints—without his anger, he lacks direction. He shrugs his agreement.

He sits, but I have to tug down my short skirt so that I can join him without exposing too much of myself. Once I do sit, he scoots away several inches. I pinch my lips together to keep from laughing. Perhaps I'm adapting to my new American home better than I thought—I'm already making other foreigners uncomfortable.

"I haven't seen you in a while." I direct the conversation before he can.

He shrugs again and I can see that I'm still making him uncomfortable, that he finds my words as forward as my dancing. *What does she know? How much can I say?* I can practically hear the questions he's asking himself in the silence of his hesitation.

Finally, he speaks. "Your mother is trying to insert herself into something she has no business being a part of."

His tone is gruff, final, but I can't let him finish there. I know better than to blurt out my questions the way my new American friends would, though. Instead, I sit demurely, my hands folded in my lap and my ankles crossed and tucked out of sight under the bench. I ask him to continue with my eyes, not my voice. But for my moonstruck shoulders and three inches of bare thigh, I could almost pass for the girl I was raised to be.

He was also raised with certain expectations, and my silence makes him fidget. *Has he ever sat like this with a girl?* I wonder. He gives in first. "Perhaps if she weren't so impatient. Or if her expectations were more realistic. She wants us to trust her, but she's done nothing to prove herself."

I tease apart the information contained both in and between Amir's words. *Impatient. Expectations. Trust.* My mother is scheming, that much is clear. To what end, though, I can't even guess. But at least Amir has given me an opening.

"It's hard for her, you know? She doesn't know how to act here. Everything has changed so much, but she's trying to do what's right." I hope Amir doesn't hear how vague my statements are. "She wants to start over. She knows she needs to earn your trust." I'm fairly certain my mother does not actually think any such thing, but I say what he needs to hear.

Amir stares at me for a long minute, his dark eyes narrowed. Finally, he sighs. "I'll discuss it with my cousins," he says. "We'll have to think about it."

Cousins. Not father, not uncles. Now I at least know something small about him. I know that his family has holes in it, too. I suspect that Amir plays a very small role in his cousins' decisions—he is the boy among men. But I allow him the charade. "You're welcome in our home anytime. I hope it will be soon." I resort to formalities in the hopes of cementing our discussion.

Amir just nods, and the silence between us grows awkward. He sits back and looks up at the sky, giving me a moment to study him unnoticed. His face is angular and lean, and his jaw is shadowed with the faint beginnings of stubble. I realize that I don't know how old he is. I had assumed he was the same age as me, but there's a hardness about him that makes him seem older.

I should be angry with him for pulling me out of the dance. What business was it of his?

But I'm not angry. In my culture his action would be considered protective. Caring, even. He cared enough about me to guard my honor. Just as the sultan cared enough about his daughter's honor to kill for it.

The thought twists my stomach. Everything has been turned upside down since we came here—my family, my head, and my heart. At this point I can't even recognize what caring is anymore. Is it the hands gliding over my body, owning me with touches, or is it the hand pulling me away from temptation before I do something I might regret?

I jump as the gym doors bang open. Amir flinches, too.

"Laila? Ian said you were out here. My dad'll be here soon to pick us up. You still want a ride, right?" Emmy's voice is tight and she looks annoyed.

Amir looks away, not even acknowledging her presence. He knows he has no part in this conversation.

I nod and stand up. Amir won't meet my eyes, so I can only hope that we have an agreement. "I'll see you soon?"

He turns back to face me but doesn't say a word. It's as close to an answer as I'm going to get. Our liars' tango has come to an end, and I'm left wondering which one of us was leading.

Emmy holds the door open until I walk through, then links arms with me as we head back into the thumping music—one more set of hands touching me, caring and possessive.

"I just want to sit down somewhere until your dad comes. I have an awful headache." Finally, one thing I don't have to pretend.

Emmy pouts. "Are you sure? There's still time to dance to another couple of songs."

"Yes," I say, and it's just about the only thing I am sure of at the moment.

WINKS

At first I can't open my eyes. I panic at the sensation and paw at my face before I realize it's just the mascara I forgot to wash off making my eyelashes stick together. It's a surprisingly claustrophobic feeling.

I want to shower, but Bastien is already in the bathroom. I pound on the door and he yells at me to go away.

"Is the king sitting on the throne?" I tease him in English.

"Shut up, Laila!" His English is even better than mine now—Bastien is a sponge for all things American.

I pull on a bathrobe and go out to the living room. As usual, Mother is sitting on the couch drinking tea. She's as constant a fixture as the floor lamp in the corner lately.

"Good morning," she says. "You looked beautiful last night."

I squint at her through my clumpy eyelashes. "How do you know? You were already in bed when I came home."

She smiles. "I was watching out my window for you. There are very few advantages to having a bedroom that faces a busy parking lot, but I seem to have found at least one."

For my mother to acknowledge her new circumstances, much less joke about them, is a new thing. I hope that it means she's in a good mood—she'll be less likely to tell me no if she is.

"It felt strange to be so bare. Can you imagine if I had dressed like that back home?" We rarely talk like this, my mother and I. I find that I want to enjoy it first, to savor the moment of lightness, before I turn back to darker subjects.

"Bah." She wrinkles her nose. "You looked exactly the way a girl your age should look. Your father always listened to his brothers too much. Their beliefs got in the way of their senses, and they forgot how to appreciate a beautiful woman, the poor fools. I wanted to take you shopping with me in Paris more often, but they convinced your father that you'd be completely ruined by the experience. I suppose they were trying to protect you from terrible things like short skirts or winks from handsome French boys."

Her sarcasm sounds strange to my ears, like she's letting her composed façade slip. I giggle—something that probably sounds equally strange to her.

"So, this is hardly Paris," she continues, "but did you get any winks from handsome American boys at your dance last night?"

I debate how much to tell her. She may be liberated as far as clothing and curfews go, but I can't imagine that even she would approve of the groping and grinding that passes for dancing here. I decide not to say anything at all. Instead, I give her a flamboyant, exaggerated wink.

"Ah, I'm glad. This is what I hoped for you, Laila. For you to wear what you want and maybe even kiss a few boys you choose for yourself. Back home things are just getting worse and worse. Ever since—" She stops abruptly and takes a deep breath before continuing. "Ever since your uncle took over, he has been enforcing the religious laws more strictly than ever. It's no place for women there."

She surprises me more and more these days, my widowed mother. That she wanted something different for me—a sentiment she's never expressed before. That she knows anything at all about how things were going back home. That she doesn't think that home—*her* home—is a place for women.

Could this mean . . . ?

It's a question I haven't dared to ask, not even of myself. I've been too focused on just surviving. "Do you want—" I stop to rephrase. Want has very little to do with reality. This is a fact I know too well. "Do you *think* we'll ever go home? I mean, not now, obviously, but *ever*?"

"Of course we will." She says it quickly, firmly, not even needing a moment to consider the question.

I'm caught off guard by her answer. *How? Why? When? What about what* I *want?* I don't ask any of the questions that race through my mind. Not yet. It's too soon.

First I need to figure out exactly what it *is* that I want. Besides, I already have an entire mountain of questions that I can't even begin to climb until I take care of our more immediate needs.

"Oh." I try to sound casual as I change the subject. "I ran into Amir. At the dance." I stop for her reaction.

She raises an eyebrow, and her teacup pauses halfway to her lips.

"He said his cousins feel bad about the way things went the last time they were here. They want to talk again, but they feel awkward initiating it. Amir said they'd definitely come if you just make the first move by inviting them." I make a show of retying the knot of my robe as I say this so she can't see from my face that I'm lying. "You should call them."

She huffs into her tea, dismissive and proud.

"Mother." Gansler's threat floats through my thoughts. Even if she's right that we will go back eventually, we can't go back *now.* Too many things need to change before we can even hope to survive there. "You need to call them."

I see that she still wants to dismiss me, so I push harder. "How much money do we have left?"

She sets her cup down with a clatter. I've struck a nerve. I strike again. "Is there enough left for another month? A week? A day? Or is it gone already?"

She glares at me, and I know that it's gone. Our survival money spent on a handful of luxuries.

"Call them. Tomorrow." I stand up and snatch her cup from the table. I can only stomp off a few meters in this cubbyhole that is our apartment, but my point is made nonetheless. She'll call. She has to.

ESCAPE

I have to leave the apartment after the conversation with my mother—we both need space. But I only make it as far as the bottom of the stairs before it occurs to me that I have nowhere to go.

I've been hiding out at the school library when I want to avoid going home during the week, but today is Sunday, so it's not open. How unlucky for me that in this land of 24-7, my one refuge seems to be the only place that ever closes. That I've managed to survive over two months' worth of weekends trapped in the apartment now strikes me as a monumental accomplishment—one that can't be repeated. I'll surely go mad if I don't escape, even for just a few hours.

It's warm out, but I pull the hood of my sweatshirt over my head anyway. It's the closest I've come to wearing a veil since I got here, and it feels unexpectedly comforting. *Where to go?* I pace in the parking lot in front of our building, doing indecisive laps until I notice a white-haired woman standing by her car, glaring at me. She clutches her purse to her chest, letting go only long enough to press the Lock button on her keychain. Three times. *Beep. Beep. Beep.* She seems to be doing it for my benefit, so I raise a hand in greeting. My gesture sends her scurrying across the lot, shooting glances back at me every few feet until she's inside.

She thought I was waiting around to steal something! The thought makes me laugh out loud even as it stings. How far I've fallen. From princess to thief.

The dizzying descent that is my life threatens to overwhelm me, and even with nowhere to go, I start to run.

It's a means of escape, but it only serves to make me feel more foreign and more vulnerable. Where I'm from, girls are not encouraged to be athletic. Our cloaks and veils keep us sedate, and there is no track practice for us—there are no jogs through the park. I feel the consequence of this passive life now, and even the brief sprint leaves me gasping. My flight is short-lived.

My only memory of running is as a child, racing down long corridors and clambering up back staircases to avoid my uncle when he visited. Even then I hated him, hated his constant lectures and his mean slaps and pinches.

"You shouldn't let her run wild like this," he used to say to my father, talking above me, about me, as if I weren't even in the room. "She needs to learn her place. It's just going to be more difficult the older she gets." I could never be as invisible as he wanted.

Sometimes my father defended me. "Laila is fine. She's just

a spirited child." But more often, especially as I grew older, he just frowned and waved me out of the room. It was better for all of us when I ran away at the first hint of my uncle's arrival in our home—his visits becoming louder and more frequent toward the end. That way I wasn't forced to hear either his tirades or my father's silence.

I bend over, hands on my knees, and try to catch my breath. I've made it only a pathetic few blocks—not nearly far enough to escape anything. *Where to go?* I regret not bringing my laptop with me when I stormed out—I could at least find somewhere with free wifi to pass the time. I'm too proud to go back for it, though; my exit was too haughty to repeat.

I finally settle on the county library. I have only a vague idea of where it is, and it takes me nearly an hour and three wrong turns to get there. I might have tried taking a bus, but I have no money and I still find the cryptic schedules daunting. As I walk, I watch from the sidewalk as deserted buses zoom past me. They're empty this early on a Sunday, but they still have no room for the likes of me.

Today, I don't mind feeling lost. Today, for the first time in my lifetime of minders, maids, and protectors, I feel a sense of relief in being alone and adrift.

But even so, I'm sweaty and irritable when I finally make it to the library. The arctic blast of the air-conditioning feels almost painful as I walk into the building. Why must everything be kept at such temperature extremes here? Americans never seem to be at peace with their surroundings—they're always heating or cooling or just constantly *changing* everything to meet their whims. Watching their industriousness exhausts me, and sometimes I want to shout out, to tell them to just *be*. But I know I have no right to criticize. Everyone needs to feel some degree of control over their universe, and supercooling a room is a relatively benign way of achieving that, I suppose.

This library is cavernous, four times the size of the school's, and the computer area is far more crowded. I feel like an intruder, and I skulk and eavesdrop pathetically until I understand how the system works. I wait until someone abandons a computer without logging off and then slide into the still-warm seat. Perhaps the woman in the parking lot was right to think me a thief.

My fingers hover over the keyboard—what dangers lurk in foolish searches? But today my quest is simple. I just want news from home. Facts and data, the less personal the better.

The news will have to be impersonal, since there's no one for me to contact. My barren email in-box is a cruel reminder of how few connections I have in the world. Everyone I ever knew seems to have either died, vanished, or betrayed—in many cases I'm not even certain which. Not that anyone would ever feel safe sending an email anyway—not from my country, where the internet is a small and closely watched place.

Without anyone to contact, I have to rely on filtered, stingy news reports. Recent updates are few; the media is content to let my country's past describe its present. It seems that not many people in the world care about a far-flung country with too many guns. Not as long as its citizens are only shooting each other, that is.

I scan and skip through pages I've seen before. Was it only weeks ago that I first read them in the school library? It feels like ancient history now. I take small comfort in the fact that the few new articles I can find struggle with what to call my uncle. His title tap-dances from "prime minister" to "commander in chief," and from "newly installed" to "disputed." The last one gives me hope.

One title is noticeably lacking. There is no "king."

There never was. It's not a surprise, of course. I've known this now for weeks. But here in this overchilled library a world away, it seems cruelly obvious. My stupidity laid out in black and white. My family's royalty was a myth I believed for far too long—a fabrication woven for a child's ears.

A small part of me understands. How does a parent tell a child a truth like my father's? And some of the lies were at least close to truths. Like royalty's, my family's status was passed down from father to son. Like a king's, my father's rule was absolute. The only real differences, I suppose, were that my father had no adoring empire and that his was an authority based more on bloodshed than birthright.

Did it start out as a joke? Did my parents concoct a silly bedtime story that went too far? When were they going to tell me the truth?

I push away from the computer. I'm too distracted to focus. My eyes feel jerky and untethered, and the skimpy information online isn't enough to hold my attention.

As I stand up, I see a familiar face. Ian.

He's leaning against a bookshelf, looking at me. He lifts his hand hesitantly, as if he hasn't made up his mind whether he wants to talk. "Laila, hi."

I smile at him. I'm glad he's here—a reaction that surprises me. We've barely spoken, but there's something about him that makes me curious. He seems somehow more perceptive than the other American boys I've met here. Of course, it might just be those hazel lion's eyes—I wonder how many personality traits people incorrectly assume from this simple biological quirk.

"Hi. What are you doing here on a Sunday?" It comes out sounding like an accusation—not what I intended. Fortunately, he doesn't seem to notice.

"Hiding out." He grins and ducks his head a little. "My parents think I'm at a church youth group meeting. I've been coming here every Sunday for months now."

The fact that he's also hiding out makes me want to confess my own fugitive status. "I'm hiding too. This is my first time. My first time here, I mean. But why are you avoiding your church? I thought you were religious."

He shrugs. "My parents are. I don't know what I am. But I do know that I've spent enough hours in churches all over the world to justify a free pass when I feel like skipping out."

He says this with a lightness I envy. Here is someone who feels no guilt for his escape.

"What about you? Are you religious?" We simultaneously step out of the busy computer area as he asks this.

I shake my head. "No. My parents aren't, so I suppose that I'm not either by extension." I cringe as I catch myself using the present tense. I don't have enough practice yet speaking of my father in the past tense. "Religion has always been a sensitive subject in my family. One of my uncles is very religious, very conservative, and he blamed a lot of problems on my father's lack of faith." I don't know why I'm telling this to Ian—I'm sure he doesn't care.

But he surprises me again. "Your uncle, he's the one they call the General?"

"How did you know that?" My muscles tense at the mention of a name I thought I'd escaped.

His cheeks flush. "I read up a bit on your country after Emmy introduced us," he admits. "I have plenty of time every Sunday to do research. It beats crossword puzzles." We share a smile as he gestures toward a table occupied by four old men with a stack of newspapers and pencils in hand.

"I wanted to say—" Newly serious, he pauses. "I wanted to say that I'm sorry about your father. I can only imagine how hard it's been for you. . . ." He's watching for my reaction, treading lightly.

I react by turning into a puddle. My eyes swim with mortifying tears, and the spines of the books around us go wavy. I'm embarrassed by my reaction but powerless to stop it. It's the first time anyone has spoken to me like a girl who has lost her father. Until now, everyone has treated his death like a headline. Unemotional. Institutional, even, as if a building or a bridge had been destroyed, instead of a man. Aside from a single anguished moment when she thought no one was looking, even my mother has remained stoic and silent on the topic.

Poor Ian looks so stricken by my reaction that I force my grief away. I've lost control over everything else in my life; I can't lose control over myself.

"Do you want to get out of here? Maybe grab a cup of coffee or something?" His lion eyes hold mine.

I nod and follow.

SIMPLICITY

Ian leads me to my second Starbucks. It's the identical twin of the one I've gone to with Emmy, down to the upholstery on the chairs and the placement of the sugar packets. It's creepy in its familiarity, like it followed me here. I wonder if I'll ever get used to the aggressive sameness of chain stores.

At the counter I stare up at the menu, trying to remember what I ordered before. My eyes are still raw from tears, and the choices are blurry and overwhelming.

Ian rescues me. "The green tea lemonade is good." It's a gentle prompt. I nod, and he orders two.

There's only one empty table, and we twist and contort our way through baby strollers and scattered shopping bags to get there. Ian starts to pull my chair out for me but then stops abruptly. He steps back too quickly and bumps into someone behind him. He's sweetly uncertain as he sits down in his own chair. It's nice. Here, now, he's just a boy, and I'm just a girl.

We're just a girl and a boy sitting at a table drinking lemonade, and nothing could be simpler.

But then he makes it complicated again.

"So, I'm curious. Who was that guy you were with at the dance last night?"

I recognize the forced indifference in his tone, and I focus on my straw wrapper, my drink, my napkin, before I answer. I assume he means Amir, but he could also mean my nameless dance partner. I don't want to discuss either, but for very different reasons.

"I know it's none of my business, but I was kind of worried about you. It looked like you were in the middle of a fight or something, and he was practically dragging you out of the gym."

Amir, then. Part of me is relieved, or at least less embarrassed. "He's just a family friend. He's a bit . . . traditional, and he was concerned about me. It's nothing to worry about."

"Traditional, huh? He seemed pretty upset when he saw you out there dancing. I thought maybe he was jealous."

So, Ian spotted that, too. My face grows warm, and I shake my head and look away. I shouldn't care that he saw me dancing, but for some reason I do. I start to explain, to defend myself, but then stop. I see no judgment in his expression, and I hear no shame on his tongue. Their absence unsettles me, and I change the subject. "Does your family have plans for any more grand journeys overseas?"

He frowns. "My parents talk about it. A lot. But I think they realize that they like the adventure more than they like the religious part. They're having a hard time justifying another mission to themselves, but they're trying."

"And you?" I ask him. "Do you want to go again?"

"No," he says with the finality of someone whose mind will not be changed. "But I don't exactly get a vote. I'm trying to stay out of it for now. No sense using up all my fight if they never even decide to go. Only a couple more years until I'm in college, anyway. Then they'll *have* to go without me." He starts to tie his straw into a knot. "How about you?"

I'm distracted by his straw origami—he's making a stick figure, or maybe an airplane. "What about me?"

"Are you going to stay in the U.S.? Do you *want* to stay here?"

It's a heavy sack of a question that he drops into my lap, and I wish he hadn't asked it. I have no answer to give him, but I speak so as not to be rude. "I honestly don't know. I don't know what I want. It doesn't matter anyway—going back isn't an option right now. It may never be." I blink fast—I don't want Ian to see me cry twice in an hour.

He notices. Of course he notices. Those pale eyes of his are like flashlights. "Emmy was right," he says. "We *do* have something in common."

"Do we?"

"Neither one of us has control over our future. Neither of us has a vote in where we may end up." He cringes at his own words. "Sorry about that. This conversation isn't going quite the way I'd hoped. . . . I mean, it's not that I'm not enjoying talking to you. I am. It's just—"

"It's okay. I know what you mean. But perhaps next time we should go see a movie together. That way we can't talk." I smile to let him know I'm teasing.

He laughs. We stay another twenty minutes, but now we're mindfully unmindful—our conversation all banter, controversy-free. Beneath the lightness, though, lies something newly solid. A connection. And then it's time to leave. We stand up together, again as if our steps were choreographed. He puts his hand on the small of my back as we wind our way through the crowded maze of tables and chairs. It's the lightest of touches—he probably doesn't even realize that he's doing it—but I feel it like an electrical current. I'm too aware of him, too distracted by his physical presence.

When he takes his hand away, I'm even more bothered by its absence.

"Can I walk you home?" he asks.

I shake my head. "No. Thank you, but no." I don't want to refuse, but old lessons remain strong in my mind.

"Then maybe I'll see you at our hideout next Sunday." His voice drops to a near whisper as he leans in, his lips grazing my ear. "I like being your accomplice." And then he walks off, his words still hanging in the air and his touch still buzzing on my skin.

DEFINITIONS

Mother is sitting in the same spot as when I left, but something has changed. Her ever-present teacup has turned into a glass.

I recognize the amber liquid inside. Liquor is technically forbidden in our country, but the law is ignored by people who have enough money. This is the first time I've seen Mother drinking since we came here, though, and I wonder if the open bottle I spot on the counter is yet another double-edged gift from Mr. Gansler.

"Where have you been, Laila?" Her tolerance for alcohol is low, and her words sound soft around the edges.

"The library." I keep my voice neutral and she nods absently. She has greater concerns than my whereabouts.

I go to my room and sink down onto the unmade bed—all three of us struggle to remember that we are now responsible for our own menial tasks, and the apartment is perpetually cluttered.

Bastien is sitting on the floor reading an American comic book. What does *he* want? After all, he is the best adapted here—in fact, he has the most to lose, whichever direction our fate takes us.

"Bastien, do you miss home?"

He wrinkles his nose at me. "Sure." His gaze drifts back down to his reading, but he must sense that the disruption isn't over because he sighs and puts it down.

"But it seems like you're happy here."

He shrugs. "Yeah, I guess." For him there is no discrepancy between his answers. In his six-year-old mind, it's still possible to be equally happy in two worlds.

I'm envious. And irritated. A wicked part of me, the bullying-older-sister part, wants him to have to choose. "But where would you *rather* live?"

Finally, he gives this question some thought. "I guess back home." He grins. "I want to be King."

"Bastien, you know there's no such thing there, right? That you'll never be a king?" I'm brusque, mean. I'm too impatient to let him down kindly. Why should he be indulged when the rest of us are not?

He gnaws on his thumbnail, and at first I think I've upset him. But he's only thinking. "I know," he says at last. "But I'll be able to tell people what to do, right? And they'll have to do it? And we'll live in the big house again, right? The palace?" He doesn't wait for me to respond. "That's close enough to being a king." He picks up his comic book, and I am dismissed for a second time.

How can I argue with his child's logic? In his mind, he *is* a king—he's been told so his entire life, and the details do seem to support the myth. I start to ask him what this makes me, but I stop myself. It's better that I answer this question myself.

COMFORTS

It's after school and we're in Emmy's room again. The faces in the pictures—her floor-to-ceiling monument to moments past—are starting to feel familiar. I'm part of the collection now. The photo from the night of the dance stares at me from the lower right corner of the wall. "Laila in Disguise," it should be captioned.

Emmy has her ear pressed against the door, though that really isn't necessary. I can hear her parents' argument perfectly well from the opposite side of the room, where I'm making a show of carefully examining the pictures, pretending not to notice the shouting coming from the kitchen. I think Emmy appreciates this, my little token gift of discretion.

The photos are arranged by theme. Here, near the window, is a section devoted to Outdoor Emmy. I see evidence of a camping trip with friends. Canoeing with one boy, hiking with another. A cluster of girls toasting marshmallows over a fire, everyone looking young and prettily windburned. I recognize a longer-haired Morgan in the background.

The next section is less wholesome and slightly more recent. Emmy is a stranger with too much eyeliner and a bleached streak in her bangs, but she's still wearing the same huge grin. Boys on skateboards flash hand signals and scowls at the camera, all early-teen angst and swagger. The other girls have rows and rows of earrings, five hoops to an ear, and some have studded lips, eyebrows, tongues. A boy in baggy jeans wears one of the *X*'s across his face.

"When was this taken?" I ask Emmy, but she holds a finger to her lips. The argument has grown quieter, and she's struggling to hear.

I move on. Here is Athlete Emmy. This must be last year, because she looks much closer to the way she does now. I didn't know she played tennis, but there she sits in a team photo, her smile and her skirt matching those of the other girls. The boys in this section wear uniforms: baseball and soccer. In one picture, Emmy and a boy sit poolside, wearing swim goggles and making funny faces at one another.

The section that includes my photo is clearly the most recent. There doesn't seem to be an obvious theme, though. Not yet. International Emmy, maybe? In addition to my foreign face, this part of the collage also includes several postcards from other countries.

A door slams somewhere in the house, and Emmy throws herself on her bed. "Aaaah!" She screams muffled frustration into her pillow before rolling onto her back.

"How embarrassing. I'm so sorry you had to hear that. My parents suck."

"Are you okay?"

She doesn't answer, just scrunches up her face, then picks a crumpled shirt off the bed and throws it to the floor. "My room is a disaster. I can't even stand to be here. Let's go to your house instead."

Now I don't answer.

Emmy sighs and flings her arm across her face, covering her eyes. "They're separating. My dad's moving out. You know what they were just fighting about? Which one of them is going to tell me. Like the entire neighborhood doesn't already know, with their constant yelling. God, I hate them!"

For a long moment I can't do anything but stand mutely. I flush warm with guilt as I realize that I've thought of her as a paper doll of a friend, one-dimensional and picture-frame perfect. That she might also have things to escape never occurred to me.

I step closer to her bed, and when she scoots over to make room for me, I lie down next to her. Side by side on our backs, both of us stare up at the ceiling in silence. "I'm sorry," I finally say, feeling awkward for not knowing the right way to comfort her. Do we talk about it, or is it better to offer up distractions? Does she want to laugh about it or cry about it? So many subjects never covered by my tutors; I've never felt quite so alien as I do right now.

She's quiet at first, but eventually she turns her head to look at me. "Please don't tell anybody else."

"I won't," I say. "I'm good at keeping secrets."

She nods as if she already knows that.

"Which shall it be, chocolate or french fries?" I ask her.

Her smile is watery. Grateful. "Lots of both. Quick."

We leave the house in search of neutral ground and comfort food.

ICEBREAKERS

Two days later, the King has a birthday. He's turning seven, and so we gather uneasily at Skateland. Why my mother chose this run-down venue I don't know, but it's a brilliant selection: we are all equally uncomfortable.

Not the kids, of course. They are delighted by the activity and pay no mind to the smell of mildew in the party room or the fact that the laces on their skates are held together by chains of grungy knots. It's the grown-ups who shift and fidget, not wanting to sit on plastic chairs dotted with hardened gum or drink from the pitcher of startlingly orange soda.

Two groups face off in the blue-carpeted room—the parents of Bastien's school friends on one side and Amir and his cousins on the other. Mother invited Mr. Gansler, but he claimed to be busy. As a gift, he arranged for the party to be catered by a restaurant in downtown Washington that serves food from our homeland. "They don't normally cater," he'd said. "But I pulled a few strings."

The food tips the balance—the American parents are now more uncomfortable than the rest of us. Even in this land of strip-mall tacos, falafel, and teriyaki, our food remains exotic. They eye the dishes distrustfully and circle and confer before going in for microscopically small portions.

"Laila, there are no forks," Emmy whispers. She was a last-minute invite, an exception to my efforts to isolate the different parts of my life. But now that she has shared her secret with me, how can I not include her?

"You use this." I hand her a piece of the flatbread that is served with every meal. "You tear off a piece and use it kind of like a spoon."

Emmy is ecstatic when she takes a bite. "This is *so* good!" Her blond-haired enthusiasm convinces some of the more skeptical parents to at least sample the food.

The food *is* good, but I can't enjoy it. Coming from Mr. Gansler, this taste of home is bitter with expectation.

Before long the kids come swooping in, red-faced and sweaty and still wearing roller skates. Bastien shows them what to do, and they are thrilled to be liberated from utensils. Eating with their hands becomes the highlight of the party, and the room grows loud.

"Who's Mr. Tall, Dark, and Handsome?" Emmy points to Amir, who notices and scowls in response. "He's very . . . intense. He's got that whole brooding thing working for him. It's kind of sexy."

I laugh so forcefully that it comes out as a snort. "Don't let him hear you say that. He'd be mortified."

I sneak a glance at him. Sexy? Amir? To me he just looks sullen, leaning against the wall with his arms crossed high on his chest, wordlessly announcing his stubborn refusal to enjoy himself. But that's nothing new. His cousins have agreed to start working with my mother again—whatever that means—but he's kept his distance. The only sign of improvement is that he looks at me with slightly less hatred than before.

"Aren't you going to introduce me?" Emmy presses.

It's a terrible idea, but I don't want to refuse her request. Besides, it's an excuse to talk to him. Something about Amir turns me maddeningly timid, and I'm aware that I have made little progress gaining his confidence.

When he sees us heading toward him, Amir pushes off the wall and takes several quick steps to meet us halfway. It isn't a friendly or chivalrous gesture—I suspect he just doesn't want the other men to eavesdrop while he talks to us.

I make the introductions, and Emmy shoves her hand at Amir. "So nice to meet you!" she chirps. Amir stares at her outstretched arm as if it belonged to a leper, but Emmy is undeterred and leaves her hand out until it becomes awkward. Amir shakes it reluctantly.

"Did you guys know each other back home?" she asks.

Amir raises his eyebrows at me. *Really?* his expression seems to ask. "Laila and I were in very different social circles," he answers stiffly.

I nearly giggle out loud at the understatement, and he looks sideways at me. The corner of his mouth is twitching, and I realize that he is my coconspirator here. We *are* allies, if only for this strange clash of cultures.

Emmy notices our exchange of glances, and a new expression takes over her face. She shoots me a sly smile and then turns back to Amir. "So, I'm curious. What do boys in your country do when they like a girl?" Her voice is flirtatious and teasing. "Group dates? Phone calls? Love letters? What's it like there?"

Amir's face turns pink. He looks to me for help.

I don't offer any—it's far too much fun to watch him squirm. Instead, I copy Emmy's expression—a parody of innocence—and Amir realizes that he's been set up. He laughs, this time without the choked sound of resentment. "Perhaps you should visit and find out. I'm sure you would be *very* popular there," he teases Emmy back. "It wouldn't take you long at all to learn all you want to know."

Emmy grins and begins to pepper him with questions. I've grown used to her trivia collecting, but Amir is quickly overwhelmed. With a sense of humor I haven't seen before, he answers until he can't take it anymore, and then he excuses himself with a weak story about an imaginary obligation across the room.

"He likes you!" Emmy crows as soon as he's gone.

"Don't be ridiculous," I tell her. She doesn't know how far from the truth she is.

"He totally does. I saw the way you guys were giving each other little secret looks." She stops abruptly. "Oh my god, Laila. Are you seeing him? Are you guys together?" She's bouncing on her toes, giddy at the possibility.

I shake my head. "No, no. It's nothing like that." But I can't explain. I can't tell her that our shared glances were at her expense. Or that I *am* trying to woo him, just not in the way she thinks. So I deflect. "Wait a minute, I thought you had me practically lined up to marry Ian. You can't switch candidates now! Besides, *you* were the one flirting with Amir. Congratulations, by the way. I didn't know he was even capable of being friendly."

She giggles and shakes her head. "No, that was just for fun—he's not really my type. But you're right about Ian. Hmmm . . . what should we do about him? Maybe he could have you half the week, and Amir could have you the other half."

I elbow her. "You're awful!" But then I link my arm through hers as we make our way across the room to where Bastien has begun opening presents. How could I have guessed that Emmy of all people would be able to breach Amir's fiery reserve? Perhaps I haven't given her enough credit.

Bastien tears through the wrapping paper with manic intensity, unveiling a steady parade of toys. Ninja action figures and Nerf guns seem to dominate. There's an uncomfortable moment when Bastien opens the gift from Amir's group— they bought him a fancy fountain pen in a wooden case—but Bastien recovers from his disappointment quickly and thanks them with politely feigned enthusiasm. He is the center of attention, a child's version of king for the day, and he plays the role well.

SPILLS

At five o'clock the parents sweep up their children and head out en masse, as if some alarm only they could hear had sounded. Apparently parties begin *and* end punctually here.

My mother and the men huddle in a corner, speaking in hushed tones that exclude the rest of us, and Amir storms out rather than be ignored. Since Bastien is inspecting his gifts, sticky-faced and happy, Emmy and I are left to clean up the mess.

Emmy is acting normal. Too normal. She's cheerful and chatty, rambling on about her own seventh birthday party, when I stop her.

"You don't have to pretend, Emmy. I know you're upset."

She shrugs with one shoulder, then bends to pick up a flattened party hat. "Honestly, I don't even want to think about it right now. Besides, you have enough of your own problems—you don't need to listen to mine."

I must look offended, because she clarifies quickly. "I mean, your father is *dead*, Laila. I'd feel like an ass whining about how mine is going through some gross midlife crisis or whatever his problem is. Mine may be acting like an idiot, but at least he's around. Well . . . sort of around."

I put down the wad of paper towels I'd been using to mop up spilled soda. "Emmy, please. It's not a competition for whose life is the bigger disaster. You can talk to me about anything you want." Even as I say this, I know it's only true as of this moment. I've hardly been returning Emmy's friendship in equal doses. My old life was not exactly filled with friends.

She blows her hair out of her eyes as she gathers up an armload of discarded wrapping paper. "I just want you to be happy here."

An uncomfortable feeling spreads over me like an itchy blanket. Emmy has been sheltering me, and I've judged her unfairly for it. She's not without substance—she's just self-censored. She's been my tour guide, social director, interpreter, and emotional bodyguard. I've been her . . . what exactly? The realization makes me feel ugly and defensive. "Why do you care? I mean, why were you so determined that we should be friends from the first time we met? You could have walked me to class once and then gone on with your life—I never asked you to babysit me." My outburst gains momentum. "I know I'm a convenient prop for your identity du jour, though. Perhaps you'll wait until spring to drop me, when you decide to join the drama club instead?"

Red blotches bloom on Emmy's neck, and she won't meet

my eyes. I can tell I've offended her, but I don't apologize. I want to hear her answer first, and then I'll make amends.

"I don't know. . . . I just thought you were interesting. And maybe kind of glamorous too, especially when I found out who your father was." She looks up, and her eyes are brimming with tears. "And you were so jumpy that first day. You walked around with this terrified look on your face like there might be an assassin around every corner. Aargh!" She winces and then slaps her forehead. "Bad choice of words. I'm sorry, Laila, I wasn't even thinking. I didn't mean *literally*—"

I can't stand to watch her crumpling before my eyes. She deserves better. "It's okay. Please don't apologize. I'm the one who should be sorry. I think I've been taking advantage of your friendship. I don't have much practice at it. Being a friend, I mean."

Emmy's tears spill over. "Oh, just shut up and give me a hug. I'm the one having a crappy day, remember?" She manages to laugh through her tears—a show of strength I immediately admire. "And by the way, I did drama club in junior high, you big jerk. So you have me as a friend for as long as you can stand it."

I hug her. It's a graceless, stiff embrace—my fault, I'm sure. But it also feels genuine, and genuine is a quality I'm coming to appreciate more and more. I shove a paper towel at her. "Here, wipe your eyes." She takes the towel, and I can't help but smile.

I have a genuine friend.

DEBTS

There used to be someone for everything. We had people to cook, to clean, to serve, to drive, to garden, to protect, to advise. There were people to manage the other people, and someone else to manage those who were managing. Our household was a busy human pyramid.

I suppose it's only natural, then, that none of us remembered to pay the rent.

Mother and I are equally surprised to see the eviction notice on the door when we return home from Bastien's party. It isn't *really* an eviction notice. Technically. It's a warning that we *will* receive an eviction notice if we fail to pay the overdue rent within fifteen days, though. Since that's impossible, the terse note on the door might as well say it's time to pack our bags.

Where will we go? I see my own anxious thoughts mirrored on Mother's face. She's wide-eyed and pinch-lipped—

this is not a problem she can outcharm or outwait, and she knows it.

I don't have to say it, since we're obviously both thinking it: we would have enough money if she hadn't bought the car.

She'd awoken one day, determined. She scanned the classified ads, then called a number. Hindered by the language and confused by the currency, her negotiations were brief and ineffective. I was hovering nearby, ready to help, but she surprised me by testily agreeing to pay cash as long as the owner would bring the vehicle to us. "But it had better be clean. I'm not paying that much money for a filthy car." She ended the call with a face-saving demand, looking pleased with herself as she hung up.

And so it was that a mostly shiny, presumably functional ten-year-old Audi was delivered to us within the hour, like a very expensive pizza. I say presumably functional because my mother does not know how to drive. The car has been sitting, untouched, in the parking lot for a week now, waiting until one of us has the ambition to do something with it.

So the money is gone. We could call Mr. Gansler to ask for yet another advance, but by now our credit is surely strained to its limits. He's unlikely to sympathize anyway, since Mother has been avoiding his phone calls for the last few days.

"What will we do?" I ask, even though I know she has no answers. I'm speaking more to the universe at large than I am to her.

She ignores me and heads for the cabinet to pull out an unopened bottle—gin, I think. My father's favorite brand. There'd been a mostly full bottle of it sitting on the table just yesterday. And an empty bottle in the trash two days before that. My mother has become a magician—bottles appear and vanish with a wave of her hand and a tip of her glass.

I think it's a lot. I think she is drinking too much. But I can't be sure. That's the problem with forbidden things— it's impossible to recognize warning signs when you're always looking the other direction. Besides, she's never sloppy or loud the way drunks are on TV. She's just a blurry version of herself. And that, I suppose, is precisely why she drinks. To blur. To make the past and the future go out of focus.

She takes a sip, and I feel myself blur before her eyes.

"Mother?" I whisper it, but she cringes as if I'd screamed in her ear.

"Please, Laila. Just let me think for a while. Please." She pulls her legs up on the couch and curls into a ball. She looks small and defeated, something I know she doesn't want anyone to witness, so I turn to leave the room. The sound of ice cubes rattling in her glass follows me down the hall.

CONTACT

Bastien has already taken refuge in our bedroom. He's pretending to be engrossed in putting together a plastic model of some sort, but his little shoulders are tensed practically up to his ears and he's gnawing on his thumbnail as he reads the instructions. I kiss him on the top of his head, and he acknowledges me with a one-sided shadow of a smile.

Money. Where will it come from? *Who* will it come from? My options are depressingly limited—grim evidence of my untethered life. Emmy has her own problems, and for once our roles are reversed: I will protect *her* by refusing to bring her into my family's mess. I'm sure that Ian would want to help me, but I don't know him nearly well enough to ask. Morgan and Tori are also off-limits. Their friendship is technical, impersonal, and asking them would be almost as bad as asking for rent money from strangers—humiliating and too easily denied.

I'm left with only the unlikeliest of heroes. Amir.

I have no idea how to contact him, though.

"Bastien?" I call across the room. "Do you know where Mother keeps phone numbers? Does she have an address book, maybe?"

"I don't know." He's still focused on the plastic pieces in front of him. I've already given up on him when his head snaps up. "Why? Who do you want to call?"

"Amir."

Bastien's face lights up. "I know how you can call him." I wait for an explanation, but he wants to draw out the mystery.

"How, Bastien?" I indulge him with exaggerated curiosity.

He's grinning, feeling clever. "*Redial.* Mother called Amir's house right before we left for my party. No one has used the phone since then, so just hit Redial."

I kiss him again. "Smart boy," I say as I ruffle his hair.

I dart through the living room to grab the cordless phone. Mother doesn't even glance in my direction. I head back to the bedroom and then stop. Bastien doesn't need to hear this conversation. He already has more worries than any seven-year-old ought to. I step into the bathroom and shut the door. The harsh overhead light makes my face look sharp and weasel-like in the mirror, so I turn my back on my reflection and hit the button before I can come up with an excuse not to.

My stomach lurches as the call goes through. I haven't even thought about what I'm going to say. Do I make small talk? Get right to the point? I'm about to hang up when someone finally answers. There's a clatter and then muted background voices—it sounds as if a hand is being pressed over the receiver. After one more loud crack—was the phone just dropped?—a voice deep with suspicion and fear says hello. I instantly feel sympathy for anyone who finds something as ordinary as a phone call threatening—the person on the other end has received bad news more than once by telephone, I suspect.

I ask for Amir in my native language, and I can practically feel the man relax. His voice is calmer as he yells for Amir. There are more clatters, muffled rustlings, and even a shrill beep as someone hits a button on the phone, and then Amir comes on the line. "Hello?" His voice is so hard I almost hang up for the second time. How can I even think of asking for help from someone who openly despises me?

But I'm out of options, so I begin to speak. I've hardly stammered my way through an awkward greeting when he interrupts. "Laila, we're waiting for an important phone call here. An international call. So I can't stay on the line. What do you want?"

I go mute with embarrassment, and Amir softens his tone. "I'm sorry. But I really do have to go. You can come here if you need to talk." He rattles off an address and then hangs up without saying goodbye.

I look up the address online. It's not far, but it's in a part of town I haven't visited before. I curse, yet again, my lack of bus fare as I pull on my shoes. This new life of mine is hard on the feet.

NEIGHBORS

The address is on a different planet. Or it might as well be. Our apartment may be small, but it's clean and quiet. Amir lives in a building that looks like a grimy patchwork quilt. Various shades of paint have been slapped on, then abandoned, and cardboard is taped under broken glass panes. It's a house crookedly subdivided into apartments, and names are handwritten on strips of masking tape stuck to dented mailboxes. Each of the boxes has a thick layer of these makeshift labels, evidence of the rapid turnover of the building's occupants. In the entranceway, a damp smell bubbles up from the warped floor tiles.

What was I thinking? How self-centered to imagine for even a moment that I could ask Amir and his family for money. Compared to them, we *still* live like royalty.

Shamed, I start to leave when a middle-aged couple walks in the building. She's unsteady on her feet, and her hair—

yellow-blond with two inches of dark roots—hangs in her eyes. The man's face is pitted and pink, and he grins an unfriendly sneer at me. "Surprise, surprise, it's another one. It's like a goddamn clown car in that unit. How many are they up to now?"

I back against the door. I can't tell if he's talking to me or the woman.

She stumbles closer to me. "Where's your thing?" she asks, pointing to my head, then drawing an air circle with her finger around her own head. "Your head thingy. The scarf, or whatever it is you people wear."

I haven't worn a veil since we stepped off the airplane. It wasn't even a conscious decision—more like an assumption: that was how I dressed there, and this is how I dress here. These people, these lurching, bloodshot giants, make me glad for it, glad that I have managed to avoid this ugly scrutiny up until now.

I whirl back toward the door and knock sharply, the decision to stay made simple by my sweatshirt-clad tormentors. Amir answers and I shove past him. "Say hi to the rest of the terrorists in there," the man calls out, and Amir slams the door.

"Sorry about that," he says.

"Friendly neighborhood." I try to hide the fact that my voice is shaky, that *I'm* shaky, from the encounter, but I fail.

"Come in." He leads me down the short hallway to a sparse, windowless room. Several chairs are arranged in a circle, as if a meeting had just disbanded. It occurs to me for the first time that my mother's little gatherings may not be the only game in town.

I hear voices and clattering sounds coming from the kitchen, but Amir doesn't seem inclined to make introductions, so I choose a chair and sit.

"Do you want something? Tea? Water? I think that's all we have." He's almost polite. Apparently my status as a guest trumps my status as an enemy.

I shake my head. "Where did you go?" I blurt out. "You left Bastien's party in a hurry."

It's the wrong thing to say. Amir's temporary civility vanishes. "It was a child's party, and I'm tired of being treated like a child."

I scurry back to what I hope is less controversial territory. "So you live with your cousins? How many do you have here?"

He raises an eyebrow; it seems I've offended him again. "According to the neighbors, we're like a litter of rats living here, too many to count."

My eyes drop. Every possible topic is a cliff, and every word out of my mouth is a leap. I get the feeling that even talking about school or the weather would somehow have an unintended double meaning. There seems to be no room for casual conversation between us, and I'm failing before I even get started.

Amir must have the same thought, because he relents. "There are twelve of us here now. In a three-bedroom apartment. Sometimes there are six, sometimes twenty. Someone is always passing through; someone always needs a place to stay."

"They're all your relatives? Your cousins?" I'm a rare specimen in my country—someone without a large extended family—so I find it difficult to comprehend this revolving door type of a home.

Amir sighs and then sits down, finally resigned to having this conversation with me. "They're cousins in a loose sense of the word. We come from a small village, so almost everyone has someone in common."

"And your parents?"

He stares at the floor in silence for so long that I'm about to change the subject when he finally answers. "Back home. I think they are, anyway. They were supposed to call today. That's the phone call I told you we were waiting for. They didn't, though."

The need to reassure is reflexive. "Oh, I'm sure they're fine. You know how bad the phone service is there. They probably just can't get through."

Amir shrugs off my comment. "Yeah, probably." He is unconvinced.

There's no opening, no invitation for me to enter his life, but I jump ahead anyway. "Why are you here, Amir? In this country? In this apartment?" I steel myself for rejection before I even finish.

But this time he doesn't reject me. He leans back in his chair, eyes closed and hands to his temples, and he thinks for a moment. After a few seconds he leans forward and stares me in the face. "Do you really want to know the answer to that question, Laila? Really?"

I open my mouth to answer, the word *yes* forming on my lips without consideration. But there is something about his question that makes me pause. He's not being difficult or evasive. I think that he's offering me an out. A chance to remain unaware. I see in his eyes that he intends this gift of ignorance to be an act of kindness.

"I want to know." I say it firmly. I look him in the eyes and I repeat myself. "I want. To know."

Amir blows a long exhale out his lips. I've given him permission to shred any fantasies I may still be holding on to from my life back home, and we both know it. He slaps his hands down onto his knees and stands up. "Then stay here; I'll be right back. We'll need that tea. We're going to be here for a while."

POISON

Amir comes back with two cups of tea and a young girl.

I'd spent the last few minutes trying to ignore the sweat seeping through my shirt under my arms and glancing around the spartan room. No one had bothered to decorate; there was no pretense of beauty or permanence. My first thought, then, when I see the girl, who looks a few years older than Bastien, is that this would be a dreary place to be a child.

She's wearing a pink dress, oddly long. It's not a style from home, but it doesn't fit here, either. She looks old-fashioned and prim, a strange choice for a girl her age, but as she comes closer, I understand. She walks with a twisting limp, as if she were dragging something heavy by the ankle. She obviously wears the long dress to disguise whatever is underneath, whatever is making her steps so labored and contorted.

"Is this her?" The girl whispers her question to Amir, but I hear it.

Amir nods. He hands me a cup of tea and then places his arm around her shoulder. He's gentle with her—tentative, even—as though she might break. "My sister," he says to me.

Her face is pale and expressionless as she stares at me. She does not return my smile or my greeting. She is the icy counterpart to Amir's fiery hatred. And somehow the cold absence of emotion on her face—it's a beautiful, doll-like face—feels far worse than open scorn or loathing. There's no child left in this child.

"Shall I show her?" She's no longer whispering, but her voice still sounds breathy. Raspy. Like a heavy smoker, which can't be possible—she's far too young. She starts to lift the skirt above her ankle, and already I can see that the line is all wrong, that her two feet are a grossly mismatched pair. Amir shakes his head, though, and she drops the long dress back into place.

"That's enough," he murmurs, along with something else I can't understand, and then kisses the top of her head as he guides her out of the room.

When he returns, Amir moves one of the chairs so that it's directly across from mine. He sits with his knees mere inches from my knees, a distance both intimate and accusatory. I tense and shrink back, remembering the way he recoiled when I sat too close to him outside the school dance. He sees my surprise, but he doesn't retreat. Whatever he's about to say, he wants to be sure that I hear him. That I see him. Whatever he's about to tell me falls outside the confines of etiquette.

"It happened three years ago," he says. "We found out later that an informant had pointed to our village on a map, made accusations. But no one told us that at the time. We had no idea our village had been declared a rebel stronghold, which was ridiculous anyway, since every city north of the capital was just as full of rebels as ours. But somehow ours was the only one targeted. That day, anyway."

He radiates anger as he continues. "No officials ever came. No one investigated; no one bothered to ask even a single question to see if the accusations were true. They just took one man's word for it, and then they dropped things from the sky. Bombs and mortars and canisters full of poisonous chemicals. They hit our school, Laila. Right in the middle of the day. A *school*."

His hands are fists.

"There were eighteen of us there that day, and not a single one was spared. Two of my friends were crushed to death in the rubble. Four died in the fire. All of us were cut by flying glass."

His eyes lock on mine as he fingers the scar on his face, and I can't move as he continues his horrible countdown.

"Most of us at least got out of the building. But it took only a few seconds to realize that we couldn't breathe any better outside than in. The yellow mist from the canisters was mixed with black smoke from the burning school, so we couldn't tell what was stinging so badly, why our throats, our eyes, our lungs, felt like they were on fire even after we had escaped. It felt like the air itself was attacking us."

Amir's voice sounds strangled. He's taking loud, jagged breaths, and his eyes look wrong, the pupils dilated. He's reliving the experience right in front of me, practically gasping for air. I want to reach out to him, to soothe him, but I can't. I'm frozen.

"The gas they use burns you inside and out, Laila. Did you know that? Your skin and your lungs. Your throat fills with blisters. It can make you go blind, but not right away. Not until after you've seen things that your mind will never let you forget. It takes a few hours for your eyes to swell shut, and then another day after that before you know whether the damage is permanent."

For a moment he looks at me with such rage that I'm afraid of him. I tense in my seat and start to rise, ready to flee. He catches himself, though, and leans back. I do too, but I'm wary. Scared. *I don't want this to continue.*

He closes his eyes and takes a deep breath. His voice is calmer when he speaks again. "The lung damage can be permanent, too. Nadeen, my sister"—he nods toward the hall—"she was trapped in the building, pinned down by part of a wall that collapsed onto her leg. She couldn't escape the gas. She had to just lie there and breathe it in, one lungful of poison at a time, wondering whether she was going to die from the blood loss, the fire, the smoke, or the gas. She was still wondering when she passed out."

Amir's eyes are red and brimming. So are mine. A tear runs down the crooked path of his scar. "She wakes up screaming. Still. Sometimes not for weeks at a time. Sometimes two, three times a night. I didn't get to her in time then, when it mattered. So here, I try to get to her fast, to hurry in to convince her that she's alive. That she can breathe, that the air won't kill her. She screams and screams until she believes me, but sometimes she doesn't believe me, and then she screams until she's choking. The damage to her lungs is so bad that it doesn't take much, and then there's nothing I can do to convince her it's okay, because it's *not*. She really *can't* breathe, she—" He swipes roughly at his face with a fist and then stops. Breathes.

"They arrested my father at the hospital. Can you even imagine that? He was sitting by her bed, not sure if his daughter would live or die, and they came and they dragged him away. No trial. No chance to see him. We're not sure if he even knows she survived."

He has more to say—I can practically feel his need to continue—but instead he just stares at me, a new expression on his face. Regret? Remorse? I can't tell. But his voice is strangely gentle when he speaks next.

"My mother used every bit of money she had to send me and Nadeen here. She was supposed to come for us as soon as my father was released. But as you can see, we're still here"—he gestures at the sparse room—"living with cousins two and three times removed.

"You want to know why I'm here, Laila? I'm here because of your father. Because he's the one who ordered the attack. He destroyed my home, he destroyed my sister, and he took my father. I'm here because *your* family ruined *mine*."

I feel a splash on my foot and realize I've spilled my tea. My hands are shaking; they won't stop, so I set my cup on the floor.

Reactions swirl around in my mind, forming a nauseating cesspool of contradictions.

I don't believe you.
I believe you.
There's another side to this story.
I'm sorry.
It's not my fault.
It's not his fault.
I'm sorry.
I didn't know.
He'd never. He couldn't.
I'm so, so terribly sorry.

My thoughts ping and crash against words that I've heard before, in a different context. Hushed conversations between my father and my uncle. Brief messages delivered by hard-soled aides. *Stronghold. Arrested. Informant.* These snippets of conversations meant nothing to me then; they were tiny pieces of a complicated puzzle kept out of my reach.

I didn't know.

My mouth fills with bile—I'm going to be sick. For a split second I wonder if Amir has poisoned my tea, and for another split second I think that maybe he should have. But I haven't taken a single sip—the cup was nothing more than something to cling to while I listened.

"You should go." Amir helps me up, guides me out of his home. *Why is he being so gentle?*

"Will you be okay?" he asks from the doorway.

I nod, silent and ashamed.

He glances into the foyer, but the neighbors have gone. Now there is only me. *I* am the enemy standing outside his home.

Amir gives me a sad smile, and softly closes the door.

BRIDGES

Mother is baking. I wasn't even aware she knew how, but that's not why I'm staring at her. I'm trying to read from her face, from her voice, from the way she cracks an egg too hard and then swears at the shell fragments in the bowl. *Did she know? Or was she also kept in the dark?*

It's a wishful thought. A way to preserve her in my mind. *Let her not be a monster. Not like him.*

Bastien is singing loudly into a microphone. He's hooked some sort of animated karaoke game up to the TV, and an on-screen avatar lip-syncs his words. The two of them—Bastien and his electronic twin—are singing a pop song I recognize but can't name. Another cultural reference that eludes me.

I tune out the noise and focus on the equipment and the wires strewn across the room. I'm certain the game is new. Where are these things coming from? Bastien is a cheerful beneficiary—does that make him complicit too? Guilty by proxy?

I feel paranoid and sweaty. Between karaoke songs I can hear my blood rushing in my ears. I'm underwater again, sinking fast.

Mercifully, it's Sunday.

"I'm going to the library," I announce to the apartment. My mother acknowledges me with a distracted half nod. She's stirring viciously, maiming whatever's in the bowl. Bastien turns up the volume.

My feet feel bruised and pinched as I walk, and it occurs to me that I will need new shoes soon. The ones on my feet came from home, perhaps the only things that have served me well in both worlds. But they weren't made for this amount of walking, and they're starting to chafe.

Shoes cost money. Money we don't have. So I try to relieve the pressure by changing my gait. Toe to heel instead of heel to toe. I know I must look strange, but my stilted new walk requires concentration. Which means that I don't have to think about anything else. I can push everything else aside as I focus on one graceless step at a time. *Toe, heel. Toe, heel.*

It's a soothing mantra, but then I think of Nadeen's limp. My walk suddenly becomes a cruel parody of hers, so I go back to my normal stride. Better to suffer the blisters.

I am counting on Ian. I *need* for him to be at the library. I need his normal. I need his easy.

But he's not there.

My heart turns leaden, and I stand stupidly in the door and

scan the room again, as if I could make him appear by wishing. There are empty chairs and vacant computer terminals, but I have no desire to be here alone. Libraries are no longer a refuge for me. The books on the shelves have turned into weapons—they're deceptively still as they lie in wait, loaded with painful truths.

A hand on my shoulder makes me flinch.

"Easy, Laila! Sorry, I didn't mean to scare you." Ian's hand moves to my elbow, jump-starting my pulse. "I was hoping you'd show up today. Hey—are you okay?"

"I am now." I don't mean to sound so bold, but I have no room in my life these days for subtlety. There are too many games being played around me. Here, with Ian, I decide to speak the truth. Or at least to tell no lies—a promise that sounds noble but will likely yield very short conversations.

I watch the reaction that flits across his face. *So that's how we're going to play it?*

"Let's go somewhere else," he says.

We're already turning toward the door as I nod, our strange synchronization present once more. Against all odds, Ian and I seem to understand one another perfectly.

"Where to?" he asks once we get outside.

The wind is picking up, and it makes my eyes water. I step closer to him. "Anywhere. I don't care."

"Then let's just walk," he says, taking my hand.

Walking should be the last thing my sore feet want to do right now, but his fingers lace their way through mine, and my blisters no longer matter. I lean into him, and we set off for nowhere in particular.

He's chatty, telling me about a funny typo that made it into the school paper's latest edition when I feel a raindrop. I can't help but laugh.

"What's so funny?" He smiles sideways and holds my eye.

"It's just like in the movies. You know, the young couple caught in the rainstorm. There's always a bridge or something for them to stand under. Where's our bridge now that we need one?" As the words exit my mouth, I feel my cheeks grow hot with embarrassment. Rainy-day bridge scenes all end the same way. With a kiss. And not just a polite little peck. No, rainy-day bridge kisses are always melodramatic, capital-*K* kisses, drawn out and accompanied by orchestras.

He's blushing too, a shade of pink to match my own. Oh yes, he understands me. The scorching feeling spreads from the base of my neck to the roots of my hair. His hand drops mine and moves to my waist.

We keep walking, hips touching, not speaking.

I hope for more rain.

Ian's presence leaves me giddy and wanting and utterly ridiculous. I laugh again, first at my own ridiculousness and then because I feel another raindrop, then another.

"Look what you've done," Ian whispers in my ear, grinning, as the sky opens up.

"Run!" Now I'm the one to grab his hand. "Over there!"

We jog to the nearest shelter, a convenience store awning, not really caring a bit that we're getting drenched. When we get there, we're wet and gasping, as much from laughing as from running. "It's not a bridge," he says, "but this'll at least protect us from the rain."

I'm blushing again, this time because our closeness under the narrow awning unsettles me. I avoid looking directly at him, but I can't help it for long, and when I finally look up, he's staring back. My legs turn to jelly. *From running,* I tell myself.

"So . . . how was the rest of your weekend?" Ian's attempt at small talk is stilted and clumsy—Hollywood's expectations weigh heavily upon us. His clothing is sodden, a droplet of rain is coursing down the bridge of his nose, but his eyes look golden and inviting, and more than anything I want to push my fingers through his rain-slicked hair while he kisses me.

He kisses me.

It's not quite a Hollywood kiss. It's tame and sweet—chaste, even—and it's over too soon. I want more. So *I* kiss *him.*

Ian seems surprised at first, but then he's kissing me right back, and there's nothing chaste about it. I wait for the kiss to erase the day before, to wipe away Amir's words. It doesn't, though. It just makes them even more complicated. Kissing Ian makes my *here* even more different from my *there,* and the nagging feeling that I don't deserve this sweet respite from my past pricks at my brain. I press against him harder, and the guilt grows fainter.

"Wow," says Ian when we finally pull apart. He's grinning again.

I don't blush this time. I grin back. "Was that okay?"

"Uh, yeah?" He's warmly sarcastic, teasing. "Actually, it was more than okay. I guess I was taking it too slow, huh?"

"You'll do better next time," I tease him back. There's a

pleasant sort of tension between us, and now we're off balance in a good way. We lean toward one other, always touching, but just barely, like we're held together by invisible rubber bands. I'm not myself around Ian—I'm behaving like a flirting, reckless stranger.

For the moment, this feels like a very good thing.

COLLISIONS

I am buoyant as Ian walks me home, and I catch myself grinning idiotically as we talk about everything and nothing. Well, perhaps not everything. But we talk about so many things, frivolous and serious alike, that it feels like it *could* be everything. We talk about everything that matters to the not-Laila I become when I'm with him.

He's the human equivalent of Bastien's cereal—a sweet, easy indulgence totally unlike anything back home. He satisfies a craving I didn't know I had.

"What's your mom going to say when she sees me?" Ian's fingers brush against mine, but they don't grab hold; the tease is more thrilling than the act.

"Nothing," I say, "since she's not going to see you. She's not ready for that yet." *I'm* not ready for that.

He feigns offense. "But moms love me! I make a great first impression." He sees my reluctance and stops in the middle of the sidewalk to bow with a gallant flourish. "Just to your door, then, Lady Laila. Your wish is my command."

But we don't make it that far.

Amir is waiting outside my building. He's stern, standing like a sentry, but for once I'm only witness to his venomous glare. Today, Ian is the victim.

Just the sight of him causes my stomach to clench. After our conversation yesterday, his presence cannot mean anything good. "Amir? What are you doing here?" *Why do I feel guilty, as if I've been caught doing something wrong?*

"I need to talk to you." Not in English.

"Hey, I recognize you from school. I'm Ian." Ian sticks his hand out, unaware that he has already been excluded.

Amir is the picture of contempt. He's an angry statue ignoring Ian's hand.

Ian shrugs and drops his hand. "Laila?"

They're both looking at me. *What am I choosing here?* The moment feels inexplicably important. "I'm sorry, Ian. I have to speak to Amir. Family business. Thank you for walking me home, though." My smile is self-conscious and dim.

Ian's eyes narrow just slightly—the tiniest hint of irritation directed at Amir. But he shrugs again, rejecting my rejection. "Okay, no problem. I'll see you at school." His tone is neutral, his wave is taut, and he's walking away before I can respond.

Somewhere inside me a spark flickers, then vanishes. Our new connection deflates, and so do I.

"Bye, Ian," I say to his back.

LINKS

"You didn't have to be so rude." My words rush out before I remember that I am in no position to chastise Amir. I duck my head so he can't watch me hopscotching between indignation and shame.

Amir relaxes as Ian disappears. "You need to be careful. Things aren't as easy here as they seem at first."

I can only stare at him, confused. *What is that supposed to mean? What does he want?* "What are you doing here?" I ask again.

"I wanted to talk to you, but your brother said you were out. So I waited."

I feel like a dog bracing for a second kick.

He pulls an envelope from a pocket inside his jacket and thrusts it toward me. "Here. It should be enough."

I don't have to ask him what it is; the flap has come unsealed. It's money. American money. The envelope is bulging with wrinkled bills. Some are torn; all are dirty. These are not the clean, crisp bills of Emmy's ATM visits. This is money hard-earned and well hidden.

"But . . ." Questions collide on my tongue, but no words come out.

"Your mother called us late last night. You didn't know?"

"No," I whisper, embarrassed. "What did she say?"

He looks as confused as I am. "She said that she needed money to pay the rent. She asked to borrow it from us."

"No!" I'm repulsed by the idea of taking his money. "We can't. I mean, you can't afford it anyway."

"Why would you think that? That we can't afford it?"

I can see in his eyes that this is a test. His questions are challenges. "I've seen where you live, Amir." I say it softly. I force meekness into my voice to lessen the insult.

But he doesn't take it as an insult. He responds as if he were teaching a small child, patronizing and slow. "We have plenty of money, Laila. Everyone living there works at least one job, and sometimes two or three. Except Nadeen, of course."

My face grows hot at the mention of his sister. Her very name feels like a rebuke, even if Amir does not intend it that way. "*You* work? When?"

"Nights. Weekends. Weekdays during lunch period sometimes if they need me. Though there aren't many busboy emergencies at the restaurant."

My brain calculates his schedule. No wonder I never see him at school. He's racing to his job the moment the bell rings. "Then why—" I search for a polite way to phrase my question. "Why do you live like you do? With so many of you crammed together? With those horrible neighbors?"

"We have better things to do with our money, Laila."

I can see that he wants me to ask the question, so I do. "Like what?" I'm more dutiful than I am curious, since I already know that the answer will sting.

It does.

"I'm saving to get my father out of prison, first. But everyone in that apartment has someone back home who needs rescuing. Airfare, travel visas, medical care, food. We're a needy family. We come from a needy place."

"You heard from your father?" I perk up at the reference, hungry for good news.

But Amir wilts when he answers. "Not exactly. Not directly from him, anyway. But he is alive. That alone is worth celebrating. And we've discovered that your uncle's regime is more open to bribes than your father's was. I suppose that's worth celebrating, too. If we can get enough money to the right people to pay for my father's release, that is."

I hold up the envelope. "Then why this? Why would you give us money that you need far more than we do?"

"We were up most of the night discussing this, and for once they included me. Do you want to know why, Laila?"

He wants me to nod, so I do, slowly.

"They wanted to know about you. You *and* Bastien, really, but since I haven't spent much time with your brother, they mostly wanted to know what I thought of you."

I try to swallow, but my throat is too dry. "What did you tell them?"

He leans closer to me, every bit as close as Ian was just before he kissed me. "I told them you didn't know. That you had no idea what your father was doing. That you and your brother are innocent. I saw it on your face, Laila, when I told you about my village. I saw how painful it was for you to hear. I'm right, aren't I? That you didn't know?"

He's studying me, not even breathing, and I realize that this truly matters to him. He *needs* to be right. He *wants* for me to be innocent.

"I didn't know," I whisper, and a part of me crumbles. I'm admitting—*what*, exactly? I'm admitting something, to Amir and to myself. I'm acknowledging the monster I never saw in my father's shoes. "I didn't know," I repeat, and this time I'm able to look at Amir as I say it.

He nods, satisfied. "I didn't think so. But even so, my cousins aren't giving this to your family as an act of kindness. This isn't charity. It's more like an investment. Or maybe a gamble. We expect to be paid back and more."

I feel myself shrink as I understand. This is no rescue, no lifeline. This is another noose around my family's neck. If we take this money, we are doubly indebted—first to Darren Gansler and now to Amir's family. I'm certain we'll pay a steep price for both of these debts.

I hold out the envelope. "Take it back," I say. "We don't want it. Not from you." It's pride mixed with fear making me reckless, and even though my voice sounds firm, I know deep down that *we need this money*.

Amir doesn't take it. "This is a long-term plan. Your family has a way of coming out on top, Laila. This time you need us.

Next time we might need you. Besides, you should know by now that neither one of us really has a vote here."

For a moment we're frozen like this—me holding out the envelope, Amir not taking it. Out of nowhere it occurs to me that if Ian and I tilt toward one another, off balance and light, then Amir and I are welded together. Our pasts, our shared strangeness here, and our connected fates give us a weighty bond.

Slowly, I lower the envelope, silently accepting his conditions. I don't like it. I don't like accepting money from him, both because he has better uses for it and because, as I learned yesterday, my family is already so deeply indebted to his. This loan will cost too much either way. He knows it, and I know it.

But welded together as we are, if I sink, he does too. I take the money.

INTENTIONS

The envelope is warm. This repulses me—it makes the money feel like a living, breathing burden, even though I know it's only because Amir was carrying it inside his jacket.

I steam-train up the stairs, prepared to confront my mother. *How dare she? Surely she didn't know what she was asking.*

Bastien sits in the hallway in front of our door, carefully sorting glass from paper. He learned about recycling in school, and he's been a fanatic ever since. I don't have the heart to tell him that I saw the building maintenance crew toss all the bins into one giant Dumpster, mixed together and headed to the same place as the rest of the trash. His intentions are noble, and the end result is out of his control.

"That's a lot, right, Laila?" His brow is pinched.

I inspect his handiwork. Four clear and three green glass bottles. All alcohol except for a single empty jar of mayonnaise.

Wine and gin and whatever else my mother now drinks in place of tea. "This is from just this week?"

Bastien nods. He looks worried, and I mentally commit to pay more attention to him.

"No, it's not so much," I lie. "Come on, I'll help you take it downstairs."

He only lets me carry the lightest pile, a small stack of newspapers. Bastien insists on carrying the bottles, stuffed into plastic grocery bags, by himself. I feel protective of him as he clinks down the stairs, and I wonder if that's how my mother feels too. I hate that she asked for money from people so wounded by my father's actions, but I can understand her instinct. She's trying to keep us safe in the only way she knows how.

After Bastien finishes putting his recycling into the proper bins, we trudge back upstairs. My resolve to confront Mother is fading. I'll give her the money without argument, I decide. But I will do everything I can to make sure she pays it back. It's time our family repaid our debts.

III.

MIRRORS

Tori and Morgan exchange glances while I pretend not to notice. They've never been alone with me before, and I think I make them nervous.

Barbaric. The word has gone unspoken since the night of the dance, but it is surely contained in those looks. Why else would they be tossing silent secrets back and forth like that?

"Emmy should be here soon. Her mother is driving her back after her dentist appointment." They know this already, but I say it to reassure them.

We're sprawled across the sidewalk, painting signs for a school fund-raiser. "No! It's all one word. Like this." Tori dips her paintbrush into the blue and splatter-writes in giant capitals: WALKATHON.

Morgan sighs. "Uh-uh. That's wrong. Look, I'm copying it directly from the announcement." Her orange letters are tidy and compact: WALK-A-THON.

I avoid the debate and stick to drawing decorative swirls and flourishes on the signs they've finished lettering. The concept of asking strangers for money in exchange for walking sounds like an inefficient form of begging, but I know better than to say so.

"Did you guys hear about Asher?" Tori asks. "He's such a loser."

Morgan snorts. "I know!" She pitches her voice low and pantomimes scooping something off the ground and waving it in the air. "Oops, look what I dropped. No, really, everyone. Look. Look at what I dropped! Can everyone see? Did you all see it in the back there?"

I smile. Their laughter is infectious, and for once I am in the loop. A boy made a big show of dropping a condom from his wallet as he paid for lunch, and when he picked it up, he put it into his pocket so that part of the foil package was still visible. He swaggered around the cafeteria like this, advertising his virility, though not with the desired effect.

"Maybe he doesn't know what they're for," Tori jokes. She switches to her own version of the cartoony male voice. "Look, it's a water balloon! Or maybe a finger glove."

"A very small shopping bag?" Morgan giggles.

"An itty-bitty rain poncho!" Tori shrieks back.

"Yeah, a poncho for his, his—" Morgan is laughing too hard to say it.

"For his little soldier?" I offer.

"His *little soldier*?" Both girls howl this at the same time. Tori has tears leaking from her eyes, she's laughing so hard.

"Yes, that's what we call it in my country. One term for it, anyway. Or rooster. Just like here, right?" I'm enjoying this, enjoying being in on the joke.

Morgan is laughing so hard she can't catch her breath. "Little soldier? Oh my god, Laila. You kill me!"

Tori chokes back her giggling, trying to look serious for a moment. "I think you mean *cock,* Laila." She whispers the word and then dissolves back into shrieking laughter.

I'm laughing as hard as they are now, my face stretched from the unfamiliar exercise. "Yes, that's it—cock. Not rooster. I always get those two words confused."

A teacher glares as she steps into the grass to walk around our howling group. We're holding our sides, snorting and crying in hysterics.

"I swear I'm going to pee my pants," Morgan says as our moment tapers off. We're all out of breath, and she has the hiccups, which makes us giggle even more. "His little soldier. That's too perfect."

We go back to our painting. I finish one poster and I'm reaching for the next when I realize that the mood has shifted again.

"Um, Laila?" Tori is hesitant. "There's something we've been wanting to ask you. . . ." She looks to Morgan for reinforcement.

"But we totally don't want to offend you or anything," Morgan adds.

"No, not at all!" Tori shakes her head so emphatically that hair whips both sides of her face.

My stomach flip-flops. *What now?* "You can ask me anything you want," I say.

"It's just that Emmy thinks it's rude. That we'll offend you."

Both sets of eyes are locked on me. "No, I won't be offended." It comes out quieter than I intended, and the girls look skeptical. "What do you want to know?"

There's one more silent consultation between the two, and then Tori goes first. "We're just curious about what it's like there. I mean, the everyday stuff. Like, what did you used to do with your friends? Just . . ." She trails off. "It just seems so different. Like a different planet, you know?"

I let out a sigh of relief. *That's it?* I'm happy to be their living, breathing *National Geographic*. I sit up and cross my legs. "It *is* different there. It *is* a different planet. I feel that way a lot."

My audience of two waits patiently.

"Okay, then . . ." I chew on my lip, trying to think of some sort of nugget to give them. "Everyday stuff?"

"Yeah. Like with your friends," Tori reminds me.

That makes answering harder. "I didn't have many friends," I admit. "I mean, I did, but they changed a lot. I didn't go to school the way I do here. But my mother used to take me with her to parties and lunches. There were always other girls my age wherever we went. The daughters of my parents' acquaintances." I'm finding it difficult to translate, not because I don't know the words but because the social dynamics of my country just don't have counterparts here. I need to back up, to explain.

"In my country, girls don't just 'hang out' the way you do here. I mean, they can't go to the same places the boys hang out. They can't just . . . roam." That's not the word I was looking for, and it draws a tiny frown from Morgan.

"There are a lot of *gatherings,* I guess you would call them. Not really parties, because there doesn't need to be an occasion. They're just a chance for women and girls to get together. To take off our veils and relax, that sort of thing. To listen to music and eat too many sweets." I try to keep my answer light, but now Tori and Morgan are both frowning.

"So . . ." Morgan starts out slowly. "You're not allowed to go out, then? Except to people's homes? It sounds like house arrest."

I feel a buzz of frustration. "It's not that we're not *allowed*—" I can't seem to find the right words. "It's what we *want* to do."

But now that I see these gatherings through Tori and Morgan's eyes, my old enthusiasm feels counterfeit. Glamorous parties now reveal themselves to have been stifling, claustrophobic affairs. But how to explain the lack of choices—the sheer absence of options—to people who make more decisions before breakfast than I made in a palace-bound month?

"But—" Tori is hesitant. "But you like boys, right?"

"Yes. I like boys." Exasperation leaks into my voice.

"So how do you meet them? How does anyone meet guys if you're stuck indoors with just the other girls all the time?" Tori is so earnest, so puzzled by my answers, that I can't take offense.

"It happens eventually." I smile at her. "Maybe not as soon as here. Here, I think that boys are a part of every group, every conversation, even when there are none to be seen. It happens differently there, but it happens."

Morgan nods. "Yeah, that's true about everything here involving boys. Look at us—no guys in sight, but we're still sitting here talking about stupid Asher's stupid little soldier."

We all laugh at that, but Tori has another question. "What age do people start doing it, then? Sex, I mean."

"She just *said* not as soon as here. Not as soon as *some* people here, anyway." Morgan lowers her voice to a stage whisper and leans toward me. "Tori's already done the deed, did you know that?"

"Morgan!" Tori flushes scarlet. "Why do you have to be such a bitch?"

Morgan makes a face at her and goes back to painting.

Tori sits silently for a minute, chewing her nails. "I think it sounds nice. To have time to just be with your friends without guys always interfering. I mean, it seems like it would take some of the pressure off, right?"

I half shrug, half nod. It seems I can only convey a world to them that sounds either much worse or much better than mine actually is. *Was.*

"Hey, you guys are almost done!" Emmy's arrival slices through the pensive mood that has settled over us. She slings her backpack onto the grass and edges her way into our circle. "The signs look great! How many more do you think we need to do? Four? . . . Five?" Her chatter bars any further questions, and I think we're all relieved.

I go back to my swirls and flourishes, and Tori and Morgan go back to their lettering. I don't know that they understand my world any better than they did before our conversation, but somehow I feel as if I understand theirs a little better.

"Are you doing okay, Laila?" Emmy whispers as she sinks down next to me with a blank piece of poster board. "Sorry it took so long for me to get back; I know they can be a bit much sometimes."

I smile at her and nod. I *am* okay. Talking about my world, seeing its distorted, fun-house-mirror reflection in the eyes of these American acquaintances, *is* okay. Their perspective is not mine, and my reality is not theirs. But somewhere between our differences is a shared space where we are friends.

VOICES

School has become a peaceful place for me. Here, today, I owe nothing but a paper on *Animal Farm*. I'd like to think I have particularly keen insight into the political maneuverings of the animals in the book—I'm certain to get a good grade.

There are small tragedies and minor dramas all around me as I walk through the halls, but they don't touch me. Emmy has tried to explain the nuances of high school social dynamics, but her lessons don't sink in. She's given up on that and on teaching me to appreciate American football. In both cases I see nothing but large numbers of bulky strangers hurrying this way and that. I can't seem to focus on the game the way everyone else does; I'm content to sit quietly on the sidelines and watch the blur of people move by me.

I like my locker. It's a small space of my own—the only one I have.

I like my classes, with their lessons so different from

those at home. World history is reinvented here—the same stories retold upside down. English class, where contractions are allowed and books are not banned, is a pleasure. I even like PE—boys and girls mixed together, their bare legs so casually mingling.

I like my friends. I'm learning to trust them. I told Emmy about last weekend's kiss, and she squealed her approval. "Eeeeek!" *Eek* indeed, I agreed. It felt good to reveal a secret freely.

I like Ian, too. He walks me home again.

"So, that guy who was waiting for you the other day. Amir, right? Is he your . . . ?" He waits for me to fill in the blank.

"Hmmm. Be careful, Ian. You almost sound jealous." Our conversations are two parts banter, one part substance. "I told you, he's just a family friend."

"From back home?" His fingers dance against mine, fleeting teases of contact.

"No. Well, yes. That's where he's from. But I didn't know him there." I want to change the subject.

"You don't talk about home much," Ian says.

I shrug, American-style. Back home the arms are more involved. Palms turned skyward, elbows bent up and away from the body. Here, the gesture is more contained, all shoulders and eyebrows.

"Would you, though? Would you be comfortable talking about it, I mean? I'd love to interview you for the school paper. You have an amazing story."

I pull away from him. I don't want to talk about the paper. "No. I'd rather not. I mean, I don't want to be in the paper.

I'm sorry." Just the thought of it makes my heart race. Why is it so hard to keep my two lives separate lately?

Ian stops walking. He's hesitating, shaping his words carefully. "Look, I've read up on your family. It's messy. I get it. But what if we just talk about your transition here? You know, a firsthand account of someone new to this country, that kind of thing. We can keep it light if you want. Besides, you're going to want to start talking about it eventually. You might as well take advantage of your situation."

"What do you mean?"

We start walking again. "College applications, for one thing. You're smart. You could get a full ride just about anywhere with your story and your grades. It's not that far off, you know."

Not that far off? Years are lifetimes in my world. I hadn't even thought about college since we moved here. Not once. Dare I? Ian glances over at me, waiting for an answer.

"Or if you'd rather start slowly, then maybe you can just talk to me about it. Off the record." He takes my hand for real this time, fingers through fingers. Substance.

We're at my door, a convenient excuse not to answer. "Just think about it, Laila." Ian lightly frees a section of my hair that had tucked itself under the strap of my backpack.

I give him a quick and impulsive kiss on the cheek and then dash into the apartment. "See you tomorrow!" I call out as I shut the door.

I'm leaning against the door wondering if he's still standing on the other side when I hear the voices.

One voice belongs to my mother; it's coming from her

bedroom. She's practically yelling, the way she always does on speakerphone. Bastien and I have tried convincing her she doesn't need to shout, but she does it anyway.

The other voice is a man's—it's muffled and staticky and familiar. Even through the long distance, the bad connection, and the passage of time, I recognize it instantly.

My uncle.

BARRIERS

My father, like Bastien, was born a prince. Or that's the story he told us. He was the second of four brothers, anyway. At least that part is true. His father led the country—by birthright or brute strength, depending on who you asked—and custom allowed him to pass his title to one of his sons when he died.

My grandfather died early, as men in my family seem to do. His eldest son died next, in a car accident. He was never a real contender, though. Too wild, too reckless, too fond of all things easy. The youngest brother died several years ago from a mysterious fever—whispered accusations of a poisoning floated around his funeral but never settled firmly on anyone's shoulders. That left my father and my uncle Ali.

According to Mother, Ali was always strict, even with himself. He was a man of extremes. First with religion. And then, when Father named him the country's top military official, he went to extremes with war.

Uncle Ali killed my father.

Not with his own hands—he left the dirty work to his second-in-command, a man who didn't hesitate for a moment when he shot my father in the chest. Mother saw it all. The killer, someone she'd known for years, stared straight at her after he'd pulled the trigger. "I'm sorry," he told her, as if he'd knocked over a vase instead of murdered her husband. She thought he might shoot her next, but he didn't. He simply holstered his gun and left the room, pulling the heavy doors closed behind him. He slipped out into the street, where he vanished into the rioting crowds as my mother screamed and screamed for help.

Word spread quickly. Within the hour, people outside stopped fighting one another and joined together to turn on our gates.

Our gates were strong. Metal bars, thick as a man's arm, topped with razor-sharp spikes both decorative and deadly. They'd survived riots and protests, kept out agitators and enemies. No one could breach those gates, so heavily reinforced with deep concrete foundations and double shifts of armed guards. "Don't worry, Laila," my father would say whenever the noise from the crowds outside grew loud enough to scare me. "They're just having their say. They'll get it out of their systems by morning. We're safe here." He was so calm, stroking my hair and speaking in soothing tones. Of course I believed him. It was just a rowdy parade out front—nothing of consequence.

But the day my father died, the guards began to vanish. One by one they slipped away from their posts. Cowards or traitors, we'll never know. The end result was the same: We were unprotected. We were alone.

There were gunshots. Far more than usual, and closer than ever before. There was shouting and breaking glass, cars turned over and fires lit. It was unbearably loud and unbearably smoky, and the lone saucer-eyed guard in our living quarters was already inching toward the exit.

I was paralyzed with fear. We all were.

And then came Darren Gansler. Not a knight in shining armor exactly, but the closest we could have hoped for at that moment. I still don't know what he said to my mother. She was shaking, as pale as the paper she signed, and my father's blood had soaked a gruesome rose pattern into her blouse. I'm sure she didn't read anything he gave her. Her movements were jerky, robotic, and she didn't speak. She kept mouthing something, some silent plea that terrified Bastien and sent him clinging to me.

I don't like to think about that day.

I don't like to be reminded of it. By crowds or by smoke or by any of the hundred things that reignite the panic in my gut.

So my uncle's voice is the last thing I want to hear.

STATIC

"It's in your best interest to hear what I have to say."

My mother is having a conversation with the devil. I listen from the hallway, willing my heart to slow down before my rapid breathing gives me away. The voice on the other end makes my stomach roil—the only thing that keeps me from vomiting on the spot is the need to hear what she could possibly be discussing with *him*.

She hates him as much as I do. More, even. She had to tolerate him far longer than I did, starting when he urged my father not to marry her. He claimed she wasn't pure enough— her mother was French, and she was not devout in her faith. She was *unsuitable*, he maintained. My father ignored him, so my uncle took it upon himself to torment her. He threatened, he bullied, and he spied. She tolerated his cruelty for years and forced me to do the same.

"I'd be a fool to trust you, Yasmin. This conversation is

a waste of time." He is every bit as dismissive and harsh as I remember. My fingernails search for holds in the plaster of the wall.

"I'm not asking you to *trust* me. I'm sure it will come as no surprise that I don't trust *you*, either. I'm only saying that we might be able to come to a mutually beneficial arrangement." My mother doesn't sound like my mother. This version of her is firm, businesslike. She knows that this devil won't be charmed.

My uncle laughs, and then his laugh turns into a cough. It sounds like he's choking, but that's probably just me wishing. "I've already taken the only thing you had to give, and I'm not about to let your *child* challenge my position. Neither of you will ever set foot here again."

"You need money."

What is she doing? I slide down to the floor, dizzy with hurt and confusion.

"I know the international community has cut you off," she continues. "There's no more aid money for you to steal. And you can't line your pockets with the money you skim off everyone else's profits anymore. Not since your war destroyed the economy."

Still no response.

"No money means no weapons, Ali. Do you think your enemies don't know that? They're plotting against you as we speak—I've heard it with my own ears. You won't hold that precious position of yours for long if you can't defend it."

A grunt. He's listening. "You have no money, Yasmin. You're bluffing."

"I don't. But the Americans do. This isn't a secure line, so I don't want to say any more right now. But I'm working with someone who can get you whatever you need. That's all you need to know."

Who is this woman speaking? I don't know this person. I hug my knees to my chest and let the tears escape silently, but I'm shaking so hard my teeth rattle. Just as I start to think that maybe this is all too crazy to possibly be true, the stranger's voice in the next room transforms back into my mother's.

"We just want to come home, Ali. I can't live here. I can't raise my children this way. We're no threat to you. Please let us come home." She's groveling. Begging. My face burns for her humiliation.

"I need to think about this. Next time we talk, you'd better have specifics." I jump as my uncle slams down the phone.

There is a long silence. And then my mother begins to sob—a terrible noise no daughter should hear. She sounds broken. She sounds inhuman.

On my side of the wall, I bite my lip to keep from letting any noise slip out.

My mother and I cry like this for a long time, separately, inches and worlds apart.

ICE

I sit outside her room until she comes out.

She jumps when she sees me, hand to her chest.

"What have you done?" I'm looking up at her, ugly with snot and tears, praying she'll have an answer that makes sense. One that can take away this crushing dread.

Her face is dry. She's already composed herself, her lipstick fresh and her hair in place. "Laila, you have no business listening to my conversations." She steps over me and stalks into the living room.

"Don't walk away from me!"

She turns, and for a moment I think I see fear on her face. If it was ever there, though, it vanishes quickly, replaced by stone. "This does not concern you, Laila. I'm doing what I have to do."

She turns her back on me again, but I won't be dismissed. Not this time. I jump to my feet and shout at her back, "Where are you going in such a hurry? To get yourself a drink, maybe? No wonder you drink so much! Is it easier to betray everyone around you when you're drunk?"

She freezes, then pivots. She covers the distance between us in three quick steps and slaps me across the face. Hard. I collapse to the floor, as much from shock as from the blow. She pulls her hand back to do it again but lets it hover over me, threatening, while she speaks. "Don't question me again." Her voice is whispered fury and her face a twisted snarl. "Ever."

I don't say another word as she walks away. I hear ice cubes rattling in a glass, and I know I was right about her drinking. But nothing else—*nothing*—makes any sense to me.

RHYTHM

Now I'm angry.

I'm angry with my new shoes. They're cheap and ugly, and they make annoying clicks as I walk through the hallways.

I'm angry with school lunches—every item on my tray date-stamped as edible for weeks or even months into the future. I had my first fruit cup today, all syrup and vacuum-sealed packaging. Is there nothing fresh in this country? Have they taken the farmers somewhere and shot them?

I'm angry that I have a visual to go with this thought. An image of bodies stacked and wrapped like the burritos on today's menu. These thoughts are not healthy. I know that, but I can't shake them. I can't escape the bloodstained context that has been draped over my life. I can't escape my memories.

I'm angry with Amir, who I saw today at school for the first time. He lifted his hand in greeting and then disappeared into the crowd of students jostling toward their classes before the bell. He was an apparition that my wretched mood turned into an accusation. I owe him, several times over, and yet I am a silent witness to his betrayal. He's haunting me for it already.

And now I'm trying not to be angry with Emmy for dragging me to this football game.

"Ugh. I give up. I can't tell them apart when they're jumbled together like that. Who can even see the ball from here?" I'm not doing well at hiding my irritation. She's been trying to explain the rules all evening, but I can't focus.

"Laila, you're not even looking—" She starts to protest, then stops. There are dark circles under her eyes and her cuticles are raw. She has no energy to cheer me up, and I have no will to cheer her on. We're a sad, slumped couple of spectators here on the bleachers.

I force myself to try harder; I fumble for small talk. "I'm sorry. I make a lousy American teenager. At least it's nice to be outside, isn't it? Even if I'll never understand this game. . . . What number is Jackson, anyway?" I hope I've remembered his name correctly. He's the most recent addition to the satellite version of Emmy's photo collage; his face grins from inside her locker door. Emmy hasn't mentioned him all week.

"Sixty-one." She sighs. "You know what? I don't like this game, either. It's boring. And it's not like he even knows I'm here. Besides, I think I might be kind of over him. Do you want to leave?"

I do, but I lie for her. "No! Let's stay. How can you be over him? He's all you talked about last week. Don't tell me his picture is getting an *X* already!" I finally cracked her code—the *X*'s on her pictures are the marks of unrequited love. They're the tattoos of disappointing crushes past.

She scrunches up her face and stabs at her hair with a clip. "Who knows. I don't even care, really. I'm just in a weird mood. My parents are at it again. Oh, crap. They're starting the stupid crowd chant."

I don't know what that is, but I can feel it. The metal bleachers underneath me begin to vibrate. All around us people join in, stomping their feet and clapping rhythmically.

We will, we will, ROCK YOU.

We will, we will, ROCK YOU.

The crowd's voice is surprisingly deep. They're growling the lyrics, and at the base of the stands an ambiguous animal mascot raises his fist in the air to punctuate. The crowd gets louder. And louder.

Thump, thump, CLAP.

Thump, thump, CLAP.

Only Emmy and I seem to be immune from this mass hysteria. *Why do they sound so angry? So primal?* The bleachers are shaking hard enough that I curl my fingers around the edge of my seat to hold on, but this just gives the pounding shock waves yet another pathway to my spine. I'm breathing fast without really understanding why, and I know that it's ridiculous, they aren't stomping *that* hard, but I'm starting to feel as if I'm going to fall through the seats and plunge to the ground below. The edges of my vision turn watery, and I can't decide whether it's more important to hang on or to cover my ears. *It's just so damned loud.*

"Laila? Laila? Are you okay?" Emmy's tugging on my arm and shouting in my ear. "You look like you're going to be sick. Come on, I'll help you. Let's go."

I allow her to pull me to my feet, grateful that she doesn't let go since the steps feel like they're swaying and shimmying and trying to topple me. We're halfway down when the crowd gets distracted by something on the field and everyone jumps to their feet, screaming, "Go! Go!"

We go. We clamber down the bleachers and away from the din. I focus on one step at a time, one breath at a time, until the noise around me starts to fade with distance, but my heart keeps thumping long after the chanting has died down and there's a vaguely electrical humming in my ears. We're past the concession stand, almost to the overflow parking lot, when I can finally take a full breath. My legs are still wobbly, but I make them move until I cross some invisible boundary—an arbitrary line that exists only in my head—and only when I'm over it do I finally feel safe.

Emmy's eyes are wide.

"Thank you," I tell her. My voice sounds far away, like someone else is speaking my words. "I think I'm okay now." I can't explain what happened back there in the crowd, but it was definitely worse than the dance. Much worse. This was an earthquake of panic. It has left me feeling sick, but not the way Emmy thinks.

I'm sick in my heart. I'm sick in my head.

I can't live like this.

Maybe my mother was right—a thought that terrifies me worse than the chanting crowd. Maybe we *can't* live here.

Maybe I'll never feel at peace, free from my past. Would it be any different if I went home, though?

I don't know. All I have right now is here, and the thought of giving up any more than I already have is unfathomable.

I take a deep breath. *I can do this.* "Let's go back. I'm fine now."

Emmy is looking at me like I'm crazy. Which maybe I am. "No. I don't want to. But I don't want to go home, either. . . ." She chews on the inside of her cheek while she thinks. "We could go get ice cream. My treat?"

"You've read my mind." I link my arm through hers, as much to hold myself up as from affection. It sounds normal and wonderful, but running through my brain is a staccato chant thumping in time with my heartbeat: *I don't. Deserve this. I don't. Deserve this.*

"But this time it's my treat," I tell her. "I insist."

THEORIES

This time it's me who waits.

Mr. Gansler is upstairs. Mother shooed me away when he arrived, so I'm out here leaning against the building in the exact spot where he once waited for me. The longer he's up there, the worse the stories my mind concocts.

I've torn apart the telephone conversation I overheard a thousand times, and still I waver hopelessly. One minute I persuade myself that I misunderstood the whole thing, that there's some sort of reasonable explanation. The next minute bloody, worst-case scenarios flash through my mind—paranoid plots and ridiculous conspiracy theories involving my mother and my uncle. And the CIA, of course. These are the moments that convince me that my thoughts are poisoned, that there is something profoundly broken in me. To think such things about my own mother, even fleetingly, cannot be healthy.

I've taken Amir's word for Mr. Gansler being a CIA

officer. He's *something* sneaky, no doubt. And right now he's in my home turning my mother into his mole. That's what I've worked out, anyway—it's the theory that lies at the halfway point between my denial and my paranoia. I believe that Mr. Gansler has convinced my mother to spy on Amir's family. She's reporting everything that goes on in their meetings. For all I know, he's bugged our apartment—maybe even with her consent—and he sits outside listening in real time. Perhaps he's changing the batteries in the microphones right now. Do bugs run off batteries?

Mr. Gansler is also using my mother to spy on my uncle. That's the only explanation I can live with. The only reason she would willingly contact the man who murdered her husband. Even my poisoned mind can't accept that she'd do it voluntarily.

She's doing it for me. For me and for Bastien, that is. She's doing what she has to do to take care of her children. To keep us from being evicted, to buy us new shoes, to feed us. This theory allows me to keep my mother. To not hate her.

I have no idea if it's true.

Finally, Mr. Gansler comes downstairs. If he is surprised to see me, he doesn't show it. Is surprise the first thing they train out of a CIA officer?

"Laila. It's been a while. How are you?"

I don't return his greeting or his carefully neutral smile. "Can you just tell me one thing?" I ask.

He glances at his watch. "I'm not sure. What is it you want to know?"

"Whose side are you on?"

Darren Gansler *can* look surprised. Briefly, anyway. Then the slippery bastard winks at me. *Winks.* He's already walking away as he answers. "Whichever side is winning, Laila." He looks proud of this answer, so he says it again over his shoulder. "I'm always on whichever side is winning."

And with that, our conversation is over, proving once more that I am the Invisible Queen. Easily ignored, easily dismissed.

I want to hurt him, to throw something at his back as he walks away. My shoe, perhaps. I can practically hear the glorious sound of hard heel on thick skull. But I don't. We need him. I know that, even if I hate it. So I control myself, taking deep breaths. I won't throw anything now, but neither will I continue to be a passive bystander.

No one will answer my questions, so I will have to find the answers on my own. I *am* involved. I *will* be heard.

SHIFTS

"Are you sure we won't get caught?" I ask Ian this for the third time.

He laughs. "Relax, Laila. This is the perfect place to practice. There's no one around."

I am eager to begin my search for answers. I itch to toss our apartment, to look under cushions and mattresses, to open, to find, to redial. But Mother rarely goes out, and so I will have to wait. In the meantime, I am learning to drive.

Ian has a driver's license but no car. I have a car but no license. Together, we make a whole driver. Theoretically. If only I could manage to keep my foot on the gas pedal long enough to make any progress. Some reflex deep within causes me to slam on the brakes the second I get any momentum.

I'm also distracted. Ian smells nice, woodsy and toothpasty—a more appealing combination than it sounds.

"Why haven't I ever seen you driving?" I'm delaying.

We've been here nearly an hour and I still haven't been able to correctly angle the car into any of the thousands of empty spots in the parking lot of an abandoned mall. No matter how many times I try, I end up crooked, straddling the lines. Ian may not be frustrated, but I am.

"Try it again. You're getting closer." He points to a spot three rows over. "I'm saving for a car, but it's slow going. Technically I have enough for the car, but it's the tags and the insurance I can't afford yet."

This gets my attention. "Can you make me a list? Please?"

He braces himself against the dashboard as I jerk to a sudden stop. "A list of what?"

"Those things you just mentioned. Tags and insurance. And anything else. How you register a car, that sort of thing."

His eyebrows climb. "So let me get this straight: you're too young for a license, you have no insurance, and your car isn't even registered? Forget what I said earlier—you *are* going to get us arrested."

He must see the panic on my face, because he quickly reassures me: "I'm kidding, I'm kidding. You're fine as long as we stay in this parking lot. But I'll take the back roads home. Just in case." He gives my shoulder a gentle squeeze. He's better than a seat belt at making me feel safe.

"Let's take a break. I don't want to practice anymore." The car seems more trouble than it's worth. Besides, I can't picture my mother doing this—enduring shaky starts and jerking stops until she finally masters driving.

"Good timing—I'm starving." Ian reaches into the backseat for a plastic bag and pulls out two bags of chips and two cans of soda. "Which do you want? We have salt and vinegar or barbecue chips." His gold-brown eyes twinkle in the sunlight as he changes to a campy French accent. "Only zee best for zee mademoiselle. Zee finest delicacies from zee finest convenience store in town."

I wrinkle my nose and just take one of the cans.

"What's wrong with chips?" he asks. "Breakfast of champions, second only to cold pizza in the morning!"

"Ugh, I hope not." I shudder. Then giggle. *Did I really just giggle?* Ian's banter renders me happily foolish.

"You're not a fan of good old-fashioned American junk food, huh?" He opens the bag of barbecue chips with a flourish.

"It's just—" I try to think of the nicest way to phrase it. "The food here is so . . . *loud*."

He mulls it over, then laughs. "I never thought about it like that, but I see what you mean." He makes a show of crinkling and crunching his way through a bite of chips, then laughs again as I open my soda with a sharp crack.

He tilts his seat back and shifts so that he's almost facing me. "I'm glad you asked me to teach you to drive. Even if you aren't doing much driving." He grins as I stick my tongue out at him. "You've seemed a bit, I don't know, distracted or something lately."

I can't argue with that.

"I thought it might be because of your family stuff. The General is getting some pretty bad press lately. He seems like he's in over his head, to put it mildly."

The muscles in my shoulders go rigid. Where did *this* come

from? I stare straight ahead. I don't want to look at Ian right now. I made myself clear the other day, so why does it feel like I'm being interviewed?

For once he doesn't notice my reaction. He presses on, and it just gets worse. "Has anyone in your family been in touch with him? I mean, I'd hope not, not after what he did to your dad. But he is your uncle, so I assume that someone somewhere in your family tree is still talking to him?"

The buzzing starts in my ears again. It's almost drowning out his words as he continues to talk to my profile. I focus on a distant point—an old movie theater marquee advertising films long gone. *Why would he ask this? Of all questions, why this one?* It could be a coincidence. I *know* it's a coincidence. But it's too late. Something in me has already shifted, and my poisonous thoughts are burbling over, fizzing and spitting like the warm soda in my hand.

Finally, he notices. "Hey, I'm sorry, Laila. I didn't mean to upset you. We don't have to talk about anything you don't want to. I just . . ." He trails off. "I'm just interested in you. I'm just trying to know you. To understand you." He's leaning toward me, trying to grab my eyes with his, trying to get me to look at him.

"We should leave now. You drive." I get out of the car and walk around the front. I stand outside his door until he opens it and steps out.

"Laila—" he starts. He sounds miserable.

But I slip around him into the passenger seat and shut the door. He stands, looking at me through the window for a long minute before his shoulders slump and he makes his

191

way to the driver's side and starts the car. "I'm sorry, Laila. I shouldn't have brought it up. I'm an idiot."

Or a spy. There, I've thought it. Most of me knows it's a stupid, laughable idea—the delusional notion of someone who has watched too many movies. After all, Ian's original appeal was the fact that when I'm with him, I'm just a girl and he's just a boy. Nothing more complicated than that.

But in my experience there are always complications. And rarely coincidences.

And my life—my history—contains more spies than boyfriends. I don't have room in my head for any new fears, no matter how ridiculous they are.

"Take me home."

He taps the top of the steering wheel with his fist twice, slowly. He wants to say more, I can see it, but he doesn't.

We drive home in silence.

EVIDENCE

At last the door closes and I am alone.

Bastien came home two days ago with a note from his teacher requesting a meeting with his parents. The surprising plural of that word made me wonder what legends my brother has been weaving for himself.

They left a half hour later than planned—a delay that had me nearly screaming with impatience. Bastien was sloppy and morose, first losing track of one shoe and then insisting that he couldn't leave until he'd found his gray sweater—no other sweater would do. Mother wasn't much better. She changed her clothes twice and frowned her way through an excruciatingly slow cup of tea before heaving a deep sigh and finally walking out the door.

I begin immediately. There aren't many hiding places, so this shouldn't take long.

Mother's bedroom is surprisingly tidy. Dresses are carefully hung in the closet, makeup tubes and bottles are organized by size on top of the dresser, and drawers contain only ordinary, folded things that are supposed to be found in drawers. There are no pictures on the walls; there is no ornamentation anywhere. Even the bedspread is plain and utilitarian, and the jewelry box I was certain she once had is nowhere to be seen. The room makes me think of Amir's apartment. It is the bedroom of someone who does not plan to stay long.

The secrets lie under the bed.

Everything I need to know is contained in a single cardboard box, the low, flimsy kind that might be used to gift wrap a man's dress shirt. I'm almost disappointed—my mind had concocted entire roomfuls of evidence. In reality, there is curiously little—a few photos and a small stack of papers.

I pull out the photo on top. It's darkly framed in heavy wood, a gaudy state seal fighting the image for attention. The picture is familiar—a candid shot of my parents on their wedding day that used to sit on the desk in my father's office. The event was a major affair, choreographed and formal, but in this picture they look as if they were alone. They're staring into one another's eyes, transported. My father is fierce as he gazes at his new bride—he looks protective and consumed. My mother is a glowing version of herself. The woman in this picture *adores*.

The next picture in the box erases my nostalgia.

It's another candid shot, this one more recent—two brothers standing side by side in happier times. At least my father looks happy. My uncle looks the same as always: ill-tempered and uneasy. Every inch of him is a living, breathing condemnation of my father. His beard, groomed in the style of those worn by religious scholars in my country, practically points at my father's clean-shaven face, accusing him of giving in to modern vanity.

The faint, bluish smudge on my uncle's forehead announces to the world that *he* is more devout, that *he* bows lower in prayer: low enough and often enough to leave a constant bruise. I always suspected him of bashing his head against walls when no one was watching—he was far too proud of that badge of faith for it to be genuine. Next to him, my father's faithless skin is unblemished—the devil's own complexion, if you were to believe his brother's accusations.

Even the clothing worn by the two men in the photo is a source of tension. My uncle, who never wears anything but a military uniform or the traditional collarless shirts of my country, used to mock my father's silk neckties. "You look like a Western dog wearing a leash," he said more than once over our dinner table. Each time he said it my mother ordered more ties from her favorite shop in London the next day—spiteful gifts that became a running joke between my parents.

"What did you know? What were you planning?" I whisper the questions out loud before I realize that I don't know which man I am asking. Both of them had a head and a heart full of secrets when this photo was taken. I shove the picture aside in disgust, flipping it over so I don't have to look at it.

But then I pick it up again. This time I focus on my father's image, searching. I see a mouth that used to sing me silly songs, eyes that used to wink at me, and a nose that looks exactly like my own. I can't find any hint of a monster, no matter how I try. The man in the photo is just my father—no more, no less. My father, with a dead man's smile on his face.

I can't get distracted now.

I flip through the documents, not even really knowing what I'm looking for. There are bank statements with grim balances and legal documents bearing looping signatures and heavy stamps from American officials. There's also a map from home, heavily marked with red and black ink, and one page of handwritten notes.

I try to decipher the writing, but it makes no sense. The entire page is covered with long number sequences and strange punctuation. Some numbers are crossed off; others are circled. One sequence is underlined twice—angry red slashes that dent the paper with their force.

What kind of secret code is this? Even without understanding the meaning of the numbers, I know I have found what I'm looking for.

I glance at my watch, debating what to do next. On the one hand, I feel totally justified in snooping. Mine is a righteous sort of treachery if ever there was one. But if I'm caught, the notes are sure to disappear. I will lose all access to my mother's secrets.

The fear of being cut off makes my decision for me. I race to my bedroom with the page and feverishly copy as many of the number sequences as I can before my nerves make my hand start to shake. I don't know how long my mother will be gone, but I'm guessing she'll keep the meeting with Bastien's teacher very short. It's not in her nature to be lectured or counseled, and she's apt to walk out if she hears even a hint of criticism.

The notes are back in the box, the box under the bed, the bedspread smoothed, and my face arranged into careful boredom by the time she comes home.

"Laila, please get something started for dinner. I'm going to take a bath." She's rubbing little circles into her temples like she's trying to unwind a headache. "Bastien, this conversation is not over."

I hold my breath as she walks stiffly into her room. I can hear her moving around, opening and closing her closet door. *Did I straighten the comforter correctly? Is the box exactly as far under the bed as it was when I found it? Are the papers in the right order?*

By the time she comes out in her robe, I've convinced myself of half a dozen telltale mistakes. But she heads straight for the bathroom without even looking at me.

My first spy mission has succeeded.

SYMBOLS

While Mother bathes, I search for answers.

The internet, my modern-day crystal ball, gives me what I need almost immediately, and my gratitude is such that I have to stop myself from kissing the screen. The numbers are geographic coordinates. Latitudes and longitudes. Directions. Each sequence a giant X-marks-the-spot. I plug them, one at a time, into Google Earth and zoom into familiar terrain. Satellite imagery turns me into a virtual tourist.

The first set of numbers takes me to the coast—a remote intersection I recognize from trips to the summer palace. There are no buildings nearby, only crossroads and sand dunes. I can't imagine why this location would be important.

The second sequence, the one underlined in red, takes me high into the mountains. Between two small villages a winding road bumps against a steep embankment. The geocoordinates point to a small, isolated turnout.

The third set of numbers takes me to a bird's-eye view of my former home. I stare at the roof of the palace trying to visualize the rooms below. *Who sleeps in my old bedroom?* One of my cousins, no doubt, though I can't guess which one. My uncle didn't allow his daughters out of his compound much, particularly not to our home, where my mother's godless ways might influence them. The boys were allowed to visit us with their father, but they always kept their distance, little junior generals already learning to condemn and despise.

"What are you looking at?"

I jump—I hadn't realized Bastien was peering over my shoulder—and slam my laptop closed.

"That was home, wasn't it? I recognize the swimming pool. And the driveway. Come on, Laila, let me see," he whines. He's been moody since he and Mother returned from the meeting at his school, but he won't tell me anything except that his teacher doesn't like him.

I hesitate, but then give in. What can it hurt?

Bastien leans into me as he looks at the grainy image. I can hear his breathing slow, practically stop, as I zoom in further. He reaches out and traces a corner of the building with his finger. "Laila, remember that tree? That's the one I used to climb!" He's suddenly animated, jabbing at the corner of the screen. "And that's—" He leans in even closer, and his little body goes rigid. "Laila, that's Daddy's car! He's there, Laila, he's there!" He's shouting, nearly hysterical.

"Shhh, Bastien!" I don't want Mother to hear. "Let me look. Be quiet." I elbow him aside so I can see better. I try to zoom in even further, but it makes the image too fuzzy.

It's hard to tell, but I think Bastien may actually be right. My finger shakes as I click to zoom back out. There's a car parked in the circular driveway—inside the gates and next to the large fountain. It's the right color, red, and approximately the same shape as Father's prized toy: a rare and impossibly expensive sports car that Mother used to joke he loved more than he loved her. He rarely took it anywhere—his security advisers warned against it—but he would occasionally drive it slowly out of the garage to the front of the palace just so he could hear it and feel it. He'd drive around and around the fountain, his precious few yards of freedom, and then park next to the front steps, where Bastien and I would run our hands along the sleek metal. "No fingerprints! You're leaving smudges," he used to say, but he was the worst among us—petting the car as if it were a racehorse. Sometimes he'd let us climb inside, but only if we took off our shoes and promised over and over again not to touch anything.

To see it parked there in front of our old home makes me feel like I've been plunged into ice water. I'm shaking so hard my teeth chatter, and my palms are cold and damp. Unlike Bastien, I don't take this as a sign that Father is alive. I saw his body. I know he's gone.

I think it means we've been betrayed yet again—that my uncle is driving the car that gave Father so much pleasure. It shouldn't matter. It shouldn't sting so viciously. But it does. The thought of that hateful man sitting in my father's car, running his hands over the leather, hiding the keys away in his pocket, *possessing* it, fills me with a rage bigger than I am. My anger stretches my skin, inflating me with hatred. *It shouldn't be his! None of it should!*

And then I see the small notation in the corner of the screen. The imagery date stamp. I close my eyes and push back from the computer, wilting as the rage trails away like smoke.

I hear Bastien's ragged, hitching breaths, and I know without looking that he's crying. "No, Bastien. No. He's not there. The picture is old. See?" I point to the date. "It was taken months ago. Way before—" Neither one of us needs me to continue. I put my arm around him and try to absorb some of his pain.

"It's not fair." He says it softly first, almost a moan, but then his voice rises to a shriek. "It's not fair! It's not fair!" He's screaming now, and I have to tackle him, physically wrestle him out of his arm-flailing frenzy. I hold him, pinned to me, while he sobs into my chest. My own tears fall and disappear silently into his hair.

I brace for Mother's entrance. She must have heard Bastien's screams; it would be impossible not to. But she never comes. For a long time we sit huddled like this, just me and my brother and a picture of what we've lost.

DESIRE

My tongue is inside Ian's mouth, and no one is more surprised than I am.

We're in the car again. I called him at home to apologize, asked if we could try the driving lesson again, maybe talk a bit. "You didn't do anything wrong," I reassured him. "It was just . . . a bad day."

He said yes, but when we got to our deserted parking lot, he was formal and too polite—all small talk and the importance of car insurance—and I was feeling too frayed, too raw, to keep up with it. I didn't have the energy to pretend anymore. I just couldn't.

At first I leaned toward him, slowly, trying to catch his eyes with mine, because the awkward space that had grown between us felt like something that needed to be filled. Then I moved even closer because something broken needed to be fixed.

Ian pretended not to notice. "Do you want to practice

parking again, or do you want to just drive around?" He became very interested in setting the clock on the dashboard while he spoke; the numbers kept flashing no matter which buttons he pressed. "Or we could go over some of the rules—turn signals, yellow lights, that kind of thing."

I waited until he trailed off. "Don't worry about the clock," I said quietly, and pulled his hand away from it.

Reactions flickered across his face. Doubt, first. Of course doubt. I keep changing the conversation on him. I know this. And then there was shyness, I think? Something hesitant, anyway. But then the corners of his eyes crinkled and a hint of a smile set in, and I could almost hear his thoughts. *Why not?* flashed across his forehead as clearly as if it were written in neon lights.

And then, once his lips were pressed against mine, my reasons changed. I didn't pull away from the kiss as I swiveled my lower body out of my seat and inched closer to him—as close as the center console allowed. Now I was reaching for him, asking for forgiveness with my hands. Eyes closed, I felt for his arms, then his shoulders, and then my hands were on his face and in his hair, and his were in mine.

I'm sorry I didn't trust you, my skin says to his skin.

Now I'm even closer, unsteady with one knee wedged against the gear stick, the other on Ian's seat, in Ian's space. Our kisses have turned urgent, rough even. It's not about boredom or awkwardness or forgiveness anymore—now it's about *want*. I *want* this kiss, and I *want* his hands to continue their gentle, slow journey under my sweater.

He pulls me closer and I topple gracelessly into his lap.

We laugh through our kissing, our mouths never parting, and I'm straddling him, on top of him, facing him and kissing him, sometimes gently, sometimes not. Ian tenses and pulls back just slightly. His hands stay where they are. On me.

"What is this, Laila?" he asks in a low whisper, but then he pulls me to him again and it's impossible to answer anyway.

What *is* this?

I'm glad we're still kissing, still breathless and occupied, because I don't have an answer to give. It is want—yes, mostly want—but also hope. Something about being here with him seems to fill the car with a warm glow of maybes. *Does he really think I can go to college here? Stay here, have a life here? Is he a part of it, this impossible future?* He tastes like hope, and his skin feels smooth and real, and his touch is so blissfully distracting, pushing everything else out of my head—

"Laila. Laila, wait. Wait a second." He's laughing a little, but he's pushing me away, his hands around my biceps. He holds me at a distance, then puffs out his cheeks and exhales a long breath. "Wow. Okay."

He shakes his head as if to clear it. "I'm sorry, I really am, but I have to ask. Um, where are we going with this? Not that I don't like it or anything." He grins and pushes his hair back. "I definitely do, but I guess . . . I guess I'm a little confused."

I worm my way off his lap and back into my seat before I answer; I make a show of rearranging my clothes and fussing with my seat belt so that he can't see my burning cheeks. "This is how it works here, isn't it? We just do what we want, right?"

Ian squints at me and tilts his head. And then he laughs

out loud. "Dang, Laila. You're making me feel a little cheap here."

Heat flares across my face once again; surely by now I'm as red as the devil. "I just meant . . ." Shame steals the words from my tongue. "I just thought it was okay," I finish stupidly.

He reaches across for my hand. "It is," he says. "It is okay. It's more than okay. But there's no reason to rush anything." He lets out another short burst of a laugh, but this time it's not at me. "God, if any of the guys at school heard me say that I'd lose my dude credentials for sure."

He sees that I don't understand. "You're gorgeous, Laila. Any guy would be crazy to turn you down." He squeezes my shoulder once with his free hand. "And I'm *not* turning you down. Trust me. I'm just saying . . . I'm just trying to do the right thing here. Because I thought that in your culture this was, like, a huge deal. I thought in your country girls couldn't—" He frowns, and then starts again. "I mean, I thought guys weren't supposed to— Shit. You know what I'm trying to say, right? I thought this kind of thing wasn't supposed to happen?"

"It wouldn't happen. Of course it wouldn't." Now I'm the one fiddling with the damn blinking clock.

"Then why?"

"For precisely that reason." My answer is sharp with embarrassment. "*Because* it would never happen back home, and because here, it can. Because here, for the first time in my life, I'm allowed to want. And I do." I turn my face to his and swipe at the tear that has managed to escape my eye. "I want to do this. With you."

Ian's eyes go wide. "Wow," he says again. "Okay. Good answer." He rakes at his hair with both hands now, and I squirm in the itchy silence. And then his voice is measured. Careful. "I want this too. But I don't want you to regret it. I don't want to be the one to make you regret anything. So let's just take things one step at a time, okay? There's no rush." He brings my hand to his mouth and kisses it once, quickly, before setting it down in my lap.

I nod, but I can't look at him anymore. I can't meet his eyes. This feels like one more example of the extremes in my life. The all or the nothing. My inability to find my way into the space between, the place everyone else here seems to inhabit. I'm either frozen or I'm exploding, when all I want to do is simmer gently and happily along.

"Are you going to practice parking, or what?" Ian is trying to pull me out of my embarrassment, so I nod again and reach for the door handle so we can switch places. Outside, the air is crisp, and as he walks around the back of the car, I walk around the front. Ian slides into the passenger seat while I pause outside. The windows are so fogged I can't even see him sitting inside.

I wish I could just vanish, be gone before the steam on the windows clears. But I've already done that once, vanished from a broken life, and how many times does someone get the chance to disappear?

I take one more gulp of the cold air before getting into the car. "Okay," I say with as much brightness as I can fake. "Let's try this again."

FLAMES

Two days later, I wake to the sounds of home. Gunfire and shouts echo through our apartment.

"Turn it down!" I close the bedroom door behind me so Bastien doesn't have to wake up to the same feeling of panic that I did. "It's early. Why do you have the volume up so high?"

Mother shush-flaps at me with one hand, her eyes never leaving the TV. "I understand the reporters better when it's loud."

Her English is fine, but she still has trouble understanding American accents. I join her on the couch as she adjusts the volume slightly.

She's hunched forward, still in her bathrobe, and her hair is a mess. This unlipsticked, anxious woman barely resembles my mother. "Look. It's the capital."

It is, but it isn't. The news report flashes images of a

government building. The Ministry of the Interior, I think. I was there just a year ago for some sort of ceremony that involved lots of foreigners jumping into showy poses of hand-shakes and back claps whenever a photographer came near. But now it looks different, like someone gave it a good shaking and then dusted it with black powder.

The camera pans left, and everything it shows is scorched and pockmarked. The corner of one building has been sheared away, revealing a conference room left eerily intact—a long table still surrounded by chairs and a telephone still on the desk, as if the ghosts of the dead were still hard at work amid the ashes. The camera moves on to show a street lined with over-turned cars that look like they've been trampled by elephants. Everything that isn't blackened is sooty gray, except where the glass from broken windows sparkles in drifts like a night-marish version of fairyland snow. The city looks as if it has been roasted on a spit—spun over a hot flame until everything is burned and broken.

Hundreds dead in overnight fighting, says the khaki-clad foreign correspondent. He's just disheveled enough to be credible, but his silver hair is neatly combed perfection. *The latest clash between government and opposition forces began when troops loyal to the newly installed regime fired on protesters yesterday, killing dozens of civilians. Antigovernment rallies have been increasing as many grow disillusioned with the country's new leadership. Now the small skirmishes that have long been a way of life here have given way to a series of far more organized—and far more deadly—attacks as the fragmented opposition groups join forces against the General, as he is still called. . . .*

My mother is leaning so far toward the TV it looks like she'll tumble off the couch. She's struggling to understand the words—I can tell by her slightly open mouth and concentration-pinched eyebrows—but the pictures tell enough of a story that there's no need for me to translate. The footage dances from the damaged government buildings to a more gruesome scene—an open-air marketplace shelled during the crowded evening shopping hours. Mundane items, dented cans and wilted produce, are scattered on blood-shiny pavement, and distraught relatives wail and cry in muted background agony as the report goes on and on.

Neither of us says a word, even as the report ends and the news anchor switches jarringly to a story about a famous teenage actress's latest trip to rehab. I take the remote control from Mother's hand and mute the volume, and for a second the two of us stare at the silent image of a posh mountain lodge sitting amid impossibly beautiful trees. The contrast is strangely hurtful—my home looking like hell on earth compared to this heavenly resort for drunks and addicts.

"It's never been *this* bad before. Has it?"

Mother frowns and shakes her head. "Not in the capital."

Not in the capital. Meaning it *was* that bad elsewhere. Like in Amir's village. "What happened?"

"The General happened."

The jagged scorn in her voice would be comforting if I hadn't heard her pleading with him just days before. Now her contempt lacks credibility. She continues, still staring at the TV, seeing or not seeing the Technicolor orange juice commercial that has replaced the news. "He made a lot of promises to a lot of people, but look what he did. He just brought the war closer to home." She sounds dazed.

"But there's always been fighting. Right?" My grasp on reality has been so shaken that I can't trust my memories. I remember gunfire, bodies, death. But I also remember my father as king. I still don't know how much of my history is invented.

"Always." Mother pulls her robe tighter. "But when your father was alive, the deaths were few. Fewer, anyway. Now there are hundreds dying every day, and it's getting worse."

"Why do you want to go back there, then?" My voice is a small, hopeful whisper. *Surely she has changed her mind after seeing our burned and ruined city?*

But my question only hardens her. She sits up, her spine stiff and straight, and looks at me with cold eyes. "It's ours," she says. "It's *our* burden, *our* responsibility, and *our* right." She sounds deranged and heroic all at the same time, a modern-day twist on Joan of Arc—maybe mad, maybe inspired.

"But Bastien is a *child*. What can he possibly do?" I look over my shoulder to make sure our bedroom door is still closed. This is a conversation I don't want my brother to hear.

Mother shakes her head and answers me slowly, carefully, as if I were incapable of understanding. "Bastien is his father's son, so the country is his to lead. That's the way it has been for a very long time. But no one expects him to actually *do* anything, Laila. There are many people who will be making the decisions for him. His only job is to *be*."

"Can't we just walk away from it? Can't we just stay here?" I hate the whine in my voice, the fearful, weak sound of it.

She clenches her jaw, and I see that she's losing patience with me. "Do you remember when I told you the story of your name? Of how you came to be called Laila so many weeks after you were born?" She waits for me to nod. "Well, Bastien's name also has a story." She settles into the cushions, and I lean in, already captive. Storytelling suits her.

"When Bastien was born, your uncle demanded he be given a religious name. He claimed it was important that a future leader have a pious start in life. Your father didn't see the harm, but I did. I wasn't about to let that horrible man control me through my children—I wouldn't allow him that grip on my son. I named your brother after my grandfather because he was all things your uncle is not. He was French, first of all, and he was generous, kind, and worldly. I named your brother Bastien because I wanted to be sure that he always knew that there was another life, another world, than the one handed to him at birth. I wanted him to have one foot at home and one foot free. Does that make sense, Laila?"

"No." I'm being petulant now, but I can't stop myself. "If you really want him to be free, then you'd never send him back there, back to *that*. You'd never turn him into a puppet."

"Don't you want to honor your father?" She reaches over and gently lifts my chin. "What would your brother be if he couldn't take his rightful place?"

A little boy, Mother. He'd be a seven-year-old boy. I want to say it, but she's already standing up.

"Achh. Someday I hope you'll understand, Laila." She's done explaining for now. "I'm going to get dressed."

The doorbell rings at that exact moment—so perfectly timed that I assume the sound is coming from the TV. But then I see the look on my mother's face. Pure dread. She pulls her shoulders back and smooths her bed-ravaged hair. "It's starting," she says under her breath, and opens the door.

TRUST

The news has coughed up Darren Gansler like a man-sized hair ball.

"I know it's early," he says when he sees my unkempt mother. "But it's important." He's tieless and rumpled himself.

"I know. Come in." She turns to me before the door is even shut. "Laila, can you please run to the store and pick up some pastries? Something to offer our guest?"

I wait for Mr. Gansler to wave off the gesture, to tell me it's not necessary, but he doesn't. He just looks at me, waiting. They both want me out of the house, out of earshot.

No. I'm not leaving. Not this time.

"I can't. I don't feel well. It's—" I see their eyes hardening against me, so I hug my midsection and drop my chin, add a bashful breathiness to my voice. "It's that time of the month. I just want to go back to bed." I bite the inside of my cheek to keep the smirk off my face. *I dare you to argue with that.*

Mr. Gansler grimaces and looks away, embarrassed by my feminine admission, while Mother narrows her eyes. She seems to be debating my lie, trying to decide how to react. It's not in her nature to speak openly about such matters. She glances at Mr. Gansler and then at my bedroom door, measuring the distance between the two. "Fine," she says at last. "But close your door."

I nod and shuffle to my room, trying to keep up the façade of pain. If I didn't know better, I could swear I heard a barely there note of pride in her voice. I wish I'd known sooner that all I had to do to earn her approval was to act devious. *Yes, Mother, I'm* your *daughter after all.*

Bastien is stirring under his blankets, so I close the door gently behind me and sit on the floor with my ear pressed against the flimsy wood. I can hear every word of their conversation through it. If anything, the voices on the other side sound amplified. Today, there will be no secrets.

"It's time. We can't wait anymore or things are going to get out of control again." Mr. Gansler doesn't bother with small talk. I feel a flush of perverse pride that something from my home could rouse this important man, this CIA officer, out of bed so early and put that twang of anxiety in his voice.

"I know." Mother is smooth again, comfortable in her scripted role.

Bastien sits up and blinks at me. I hold a finger to my lips, and he nods and crawls silently over. He pulls his knees up to his chest and leans against me, his little body warm and trusting. He doesn't look surprised to find me eavesdropping—I can't decide whether this says more about him or me.

"We're not interested in simply delaying the inevitable, Yasmin. If he can't hang on to power, then there's no sense in backing him. And frankly, I'm not convinced he's even going to play ball. We sit on different sides of a pretty high ideological fence." Mr. Gansler sounds peevish, like a man who needs a strong cup of coffee before dealing with this mess. I wonder whether he has a wife, and what he tells her when he rushes off. *Don't hold dinner, dear, I might be late. We're launching a civil war today—you know how it is.*

"*You* control the money, so *you* control the outcome, Darren. His grip on power may be shaky right now, but it's not too late to reverse things. Besides, if you decide to back someone else you're going to have to start from scratch. There *is* no one else with a chance of uniting the factions. The General may not be the best choice, but right now he is the *only* choice." Her voice is low, convincing. Almost hypnotic.

For the first time I wonder how much of a role she played in my father's decisions. She is, after all, calmly negotiating support for the man who killed her husband. Did she ever use that same lulling tone to suggest a bombing campaign? Did she speak with such smooth confidence while listing the virtues of using chemical weapons against unsuspecting villagers? Against children?

Stop! I have to purge these thoughts from my head. They're distracting me. Bastien fidgets, trying to get more comfortable against me, and I force myself to focus.

"He'll listen to me, Darren. I'll make the arrangements. Just promise me that you'll deliver the money personally. I can't vouch for anyone else, but I know that I can vouch for

215

you. I trust you—you know what's at stake better than anyone else in Washington. You've been there. You know what it's like."

Nice touch, Mother. I feel dirty listening to her shamelessly manipulate him. I'm certain he'll see through it.

But apparently he doesn't.

"We need to move fast. It's a lot of money, Yasmin. A *lot* of money. Make sure he understands the obligations that come with it."

"He'll understand."

I hear them moving, the front door opening, an exchange of goodbyes, and then nothing. I crack my bedroom door open silently, slowly, nudging Bastien aside so I can peer out.

My mother, master manipulator and careful plotter, is standing with her back against the front door. Her face is pale, and her lips are pressed together like they're barely containing a scream. She is a hurting, haunted shell.

Good. Let her hurt. The anger that jumps unbidden into my mind scares me. It feels like a point of no return. But if I'm hurting, she should be too.

She opens her eyes and looks right at me. For several long seconds we're frozen, staring at each other, and somehow I become the guilty party. I drop my eyes, ashamed, but I feel her continue to stare. I don't look up until I hear the ice cubes tinkling into the glass and the sounds of my mother, still in her nightclothes, pouring herself a drink.

ATTENTION

The news holds us prisoner while the sun rises outside. Slashes of morning light enter our apartment through the gaps of our still-closed blinds, but none of us get up to open the shades.

We sit, glassy-eyed, waiting for the revolving-door news channel to get back to the story. Four minutes of commercials to three minutes of news; snippets of home in hyperactive forty-five-second bursts only every so often. Mother swirls the ice in her otherwise empty glass, and the cubes rattle like boozy castanets until they melt. Bastien is on the couch next to her with his hands hovering slyly near his mouth. When he thinks no one is watching, he sucks his thumb the way he used to when he was younger. He turns it into nail biting the moment anyone looks, which he seems to think is a more acceptable vice for a seven-year-old.

I'm too impatient for the teases and the snippets, so I turn on my computer. I have to wade through several layers of reports—the rehab starlet has already checked herself out!—before I find what I'm looking for. The news is not good. Retaliation has begun, and the death toll is climbing. The General has gone on the offensive, and the provinces are suffering his wrath.

My first thought as I read this is of Amir. Is that strange? I search, and I'm relieved to find no mention of his village.

"Laila, are we going to school today?" Bastien has abandoned his news vigil, and now he's restless.

I glance at the clock. We're already late. "Yes, let's go. We might as well—there's no new information anyway. Get dressed, quick."

Bastien skitters off without protest.

Mother barely acknowledges our scurried attempts to get ready for school, but she stops me as we're rushing out the door. "Laila, wait. I need you to do something for me." She steps into her bedroom, then emerges with a thick envelope. "Give this to your friend, please. What's his name, Amir? It's the money we borrowed."

My friend? And his name so easily forgotten? "Where did you get this? I thought we were broke. And why don't you give it to his cousins the next time you see them?"

She frowns at my questions and pushes the envelope at me. "Laila, please. Just do as I ask. We have plenty of money now; we won't need to borrow from them again. And I don't think I'll be seeing anyone from that family anytime soon."

This has something to do with the news. With Mr. Gansler's visit. With my uncle. "Why?" I ask, not expecting a response.

She surprises me with a half answer, which is half more than I expected. "Darren's interests have shifted, and he's the one who pays the bills." She shoos us off and shuts the door before I can ask anything else.

I walk Bastien to his school. It's out of my way, but late as I am already, another twenty minutes doesn't matter.

He straddles the curb as he walks, one foot on the sidewalk and one on the street. It gives him a lurching gait that makes me think of Amir's sister. "Bastien, why did your teacher ask to meet with Mother?"

He scowls and kicks at a rock. "She says I'm lying. She says I make things up."

I know immediately what he has been lying about, and my heart aches for him. "Did you tell people you're a king?" I ask softly.

He looks at his feet and bobs his head in the tiniest of nods.

I start to tell him he shouldn't say such things, that it isn't true, but I stop myself. Who am I to say what's true? Mother has dragged us both into a game I don't understand. For all I know, Bastien *will* be king once she's done maneuvering. And if not, our future is a bleak question mark. Bastien's stories may be the only things that survive intact.

I shudder and walk faster. "Hurry up," I snap at Bastien, and he looks relieved the conversation is over.

ALARMS

I arrive at school to find that my Here and my There have collided.

Cars and trucks with flashing lights crowd the street, and somewhere inside a tinny alarm sounds, on and on and on. Icy fingers of panic caress and then start to claw at my chest. My first thought is that the war has followed me, encircled my life completely.

Then I notice the other students.

They're milling around the front entrance in a boisterous crowd, their expressions falling within a narrow range from neutral to cheerful. At worst, some look bored. There is no crying; there are no screams. But I still can't push away the piercing dread that something terrible has happened.

I find Emmy standing near one of the fire trucks. She bounces up and down on her toes and waves with both hands when she sees me. "Laila! Where have you been? Have you heard the good news? Someone called in a bomb threat!"

I'm certain I heard wrong—I'm so distracted by the red-white-red-white lights dancing across her face that I can't grasp the meaning of her words. "What?"

"Bomb threat! Woo-hoo!" Someone in the crowd yells it, and then someone else tries to start a chant. "Make the call! Make the call!" It doesn't catch on, but I can't stop myself from taking a step back, away from the shouting. I stumble over the curb, falling in a clumsy heap.

"Oh, Laila." Emmy's eyes go wide and she covers her mouth with a hand. "I didn't even think." She rushes over and pulls me up. "Don't worry. It's not a real bomb—it never is. This happens at least once a year, but usually not until the weather's nicer, or on Senior Skip Day. We're just waiting until the principal makes the call—he has to officially make the decision to evacuate the school for the day. Which *always* happens."

I understand her this time, but it doesn't keep me from wishing we could move just a little farther away from the building, farther away from the flashing lights. Just in case. "But what if—?" The alarm clanging in the background cuts off abruptly, and the students cheer.

Emmy's bouncing on her toes again, but she keeps a tight grip on me. "Okay, that probably means he's about to make the announcement. Shhh. Listen."

The sound of a man clearing his throat comes out of the loudspeakers, and then a decidedly unpanicked voice announces that the school is being evacuated for the remainder of the day. He says something about alternate locations being set up for use as study halls, and the crowd jeers.

"This is sick," I say, but no one hears me. Emmy is laughing along with everyone else. "You people are sick."

"Let's go find Tori and Morgan," Emmy says, pulling me along with her. "Everyone's heading to the park now—we should hurry so we can get a good spot on the hill."

I'm too disoriented to do anything but follow.

STORM

"This is exactly why these things aren't supposed to happen until spring, people!" Morgan shouts to no one in particular. "I'm freezing!"

My friends are disappointed with their day at the park. Their bomb has bombed. It's cold out, and the scrubby grass on the hill where dozens of students have come to gather is damp. Grope Slope, they call this place, and it's easy to understand why. The dreary conditions have not discouraged the public displays of affection that began to blossom around us, particularly after one entrepreneurial student showed up with a cooler and started to discreetly sell cans of beer. It's a meaningless tradition, Tori explains. A way to pass the time.

"This place is kind of like mistletoe," Morgan tries to clarify. "The kisses don't really count."

"It's stupid." Emmy wrinkles her nose as she shifts her weight and the plastic garbage bag we're using as a picnic blanket crinkles and sticks to her legs. "This whole day sucks." Her eyes scan constantly, searching for someone who was supposed to be here but isn't. Her next photo op, waiting to happen.

Her mood is all peaks and valleys today, and I can't do a thing to cheer her. My mind is anywhere but here—my thoughts focus on bombs that are not pretend, while hers swirl around a boy who did not come. Today our differences form a perfect storm, and now she heaves deep, theatrical sighs and stabs at the uneaten take-out salad we are supposed to be sharing. She's waiting for me to notice that she's mad.

Emmy, the least angry person I've ever met, is angry with me. The only surprise is that it's taken this long. Finally, I grant her my full attention.

"What wrong?"

"Nothing. It's just . . . you've been kind of flaky lately." She's hesitant at first, but then her words come out in a rush. "I know you have stuff going on in your life, but I do too. Not that you seem to care. And what's going on with Ian, anyway? He told me he's worried about you, but he won't say why. And since you've barely spoken to me this week, what would I know?" It sounds like she's been holding this in for days. She probably has. Not that I would have noticed—she's right about that. The events of the last few days have eclipsed everything else around me—including Emmy. I try to muster something pleasantly distracting to say, but it backfires.

"You think this is funny?" Emmy's eyes go wide, her anger now edged with hurt.

"No, no. I'm sorry. That's not why I was smiling. I'm

just . . . I don't know. Stressed out. I was just thinking that *flaky* is such a strange word to use. In my mind, flaky is a good thing—it's a perfect pastry." I'm fumbling. I *am* flaky.

"No. Don't pull that lost-in-translation crap, Laila. A friend is a friend in any language. Just like a jerk is a jerk." She pushes away from our garbage-bag picnic and weaves her way through the other clusters of students sitting on the hillside.

I know I should go after her, but I don't. I can't. I just don't have the energy. I care about Emmy, I truly do. But I can't care as much as she wants right now. Not with everything else going on in my life. I have tunnel vision, and Emmy stands outside the tunnel. She's better off that way, even if she doesn't think so.

Tori and Morgan are silent, which probably means my flakiness has been an earlier topic of conversation. We sit without words until Ian joins us, taking Emmy's place on our sad plastic picnic blanket.

He's tentative as he sits down, mumbling a polite greeting to the group and then turning to me. "You doing okay?" he asks.

I nod, but I can't even feign a smile. Emmy's departure has rattled me, left me anchorless in this place that only days ago had started to seem safe and familiar. "Happy bomb threat day," I say. I don't disguise the bitterness in my voice, but Ian puts his arm around me anyway.

"Ugh, not you guys too," Morgan groans. "I can't take any more Grope Slope today. I'm outta here."

Tori jumps up with her. "See you guys later," she says, winking suggestively at us before she leaves.

Everything about today makes me queasy and miserable. I'm trying to appreciate Ian's kindness. I'm glad that he's forgiven my behavior in the car, but when he leans over and nuzzles the underside of my jaw, I feel no less queasy or miserable than before, and I'm relieved when he stops.

"This *is* pretty lame," Ian echoes Morgan. "Do you want to go get some coffee or something? You look cold."

I start to say yes automatically, but then I stop myself. I don't want coffee. I don't want to sit here in celebration of someone claiming to have planted a bomb in a school, either. I'm half shivering, half burning up, and I'm half outraged and half numb. I'm half Here. I'm half There. I'm a girl divided, which is to say that I'm no one at all.

"No." I shake my head. I'm going to say more, but the words don't come. All I can think about is Amir, and what must have gone through his head when he heard about a bomb in his school—what panicked memories must have spilled from his heart.

Ian pulls away from me, and the muscles in his jaw bunch up. "Laila, I can't figure you out. One day you're all over me, and the next it's like you can't even stand me."

"I'm sorry," I say to the patch of weeds growing at my feet.

He softens. "It's okay. I know there's all sorts of shit going on back home for you right now."

"No, Ian. I'm sorry for more than just today. I'm sorry because . . . because I can't. Any of this. You. Here." I'm babbling as I push to my feet. My words are unplanned and surprise me as much as they surprise him. "I just don't *work* here. There's something wrong with me here."

He reaches for my hand. "Laila, let me do something. Let me help you."

But I shake my head again and pull my hand back. "There's nothing you can do, Ian." I kiss his cheek once, quickly, and then I race away.

I need to find Amir.

THRESHOLD

I don't know where to start.

He's not at school, of course. The evacuation orders were real, even if the bomb was not. I think about finding a phone to call his home, but I'm stopped by tumbling, troubling images of people packed into Amir's apartment watching the news, waiting for news. In my mind, his sister sits too close to the television, afraid to glance away in case a crowd scene contains someone she knows. I imagine her crying as she watches. Others in the room cry too, either because they fear the worst or because they already know the worst. My eyes burn at the thought—I can't call there.

Work. With no school today, maybe Amir went to work? I can hardly walk fast enough—I practically run the blocks between the park and the restaurant where he washes dishes and takes out garbage. I've never been inside, but I've walked past it a hundred times.

"Here for a late lunch?" A bulldog-faced man in a stained apron greets me from behind the counter.

"No. I'm looking for Amir. Is he working right now?"

The man scowls. "Yeah. He's *working*." His emphasis is meant to deter me.

"Please. It will be just for a moment." My princess voice is rusty, but it works.

The scowling man relents. "Amir!"

No response. He grumbles before turning on his heel to check the back room. When he returns, he busies himself wiping the counter with a filthy rag, making me wait for his answer. "He'll be out in a minute. *For* a minute," he says finally. I nod and wait by the door.

I want to know that he's okay. That the bomb threat didn't take him back to his past, reviving memories better left buried. As far as I know, Amir doesn't have any American friends—no one like Emmy to explain the joke. He has no context for a celebrated threat.

But I also have another reason. A selfish one.

I want to see his face when I pay back the money. I want to watch him as I hand over the envelope, to see if he understands whatever it is that has changed any better than I do. So much will depend on his reaction.

So far, this is what I believe: My mother *does* hate my uncle. But she also has a plan. A goal. And her desire to achieve it outweighs her hatred. My mother will deal with the devil, it seems, to get what she wants. But I'm still hoping a tiny, foolish hope that Amir will somehow be able to interpret things differently. That he can find goodness where I see only betrayal.

Amir comes out of the kitchen, and we both ignore the bulldog man as we step outside to talk. He gestures to a flimsy table, and we sit down across from one another.

"Are you okay?" I ask him without any greeting. "I mean, the thing at school . . . ?"

He grunts dismissively. "People here can be so stupid. It's like a game to them."

For the first time all week, I smile. Finally, someone sees the events of the day the same way I do.

But Amir isn't smiling. "You've seen the news? From home?"

He's worried. Just like I am. He's jumpy, and his eyes are bloodshot and sunken as if he hasn't slept in days. We're two people with the same worries, a sorry fact that for a moment makes me want to embrace him. But then I remember that our worries are *not* entirely the same. Same facts, very different context.

"Yes. We've been watching—it's awful. How is your family? The ones back home, I mean. Are they okay?"

He lets out a long puff of air. He holds his breath when he's nervous, just like I do. "I don't know. We haven't heard of any strikes in our area, but we can't be sure. The news is slow to catch up, and the phones aren't working. I went home to check in after the school was evacuated, but I couldn't stand waiting around anymore, so I came here."

I reach over and place my hand on his, then immediately feel self-conscious. But he doesn't even seem to notice, so I leave my hand there. It's an American gesture, this casual

230

touch across genders, but it feels natural to reach out to him right now. There's no tension, no power play. Just a much-needed connection.

"The capital was hit pretty hard. Do you . . . do you have anyone there still? Is *your* family safe?" He words his questions carefully so we aren't forced to admit out loud that we have family on opposite sides of the fighting.

I shake my head. "There's no one left there." We reach an unspoken agreement that my tie to the General will not be recognized. "What about your father? Do you have any news about him?"

"I can't believe I haven't told you already." A grin spreads across his face. "He's out! He's out of prison. We got enough money to the right people, the stars aligned, and he's home. With my mother. Just in time, it seems. I don't even want to think what would have happened if we'd waited any longer, now that the fighting has started."

"I'm so happy for you, Amir. I really am. I'm glad every-thing worked out."

His smile falters. "Well, he's missing half his fingernails and a third of his body weight, but he'll heal. Eventually."

An awkward silence wedges itself between us. I'd read about the prisons. About how many people went in and how few came out. It was one of the articles that sparked my deci-sion to stay out of libraries.

The lack of words, my inability to say anything remotely appropriate, is almost physically painful. Finally, I remember the money. I pull the envelope from my backpack, grateful for any sort of diversion. "I have money for you. To pay back your family. I hope that loaning it to us didn't keep you from getting your father home sooner."

Amir doesn't move as he stares at my hand. He has turned to stone.

Finally, slowly, one corner of his mouth turns up in a grim not-smile, and he reaches to take the money. "That was quick," he says in a flat voice. He glances at the bills. "We haven't heard from your mother for a while. I guess this explains why."

I know I'm supposed to act like I understand what's going on, that I shouldn't admit my ignorance to Amir, but I don't even know why that is. Mother was the one who first threw me together with him, a boy I never would have crossed paths with back home. Someone who would have been invisible to me, and if not invisible, then forbidden. Back home my family was Us and everyone else was Them. But the lines have all blurred, and here, Amir is one of Us. At least, he *was*. Briefly, we were on the same team, even if I never knew which game we were playing. *How am I supposed to keep up with the changes when I don't understand the rules?*

"What does it explain, Amir?" My voice cracks, and suddenly I'm crying, though not from sadness. This time it's because I'm just so . . . tired. I have an overwhelming impulse to crawl under the table and lie in fetal position, to sleep like that, lulled by the sounds of normal lives all around me. "I know the money comes from Mr. Gansler, and I know who he is. What he is. But what does it *mean*?"

He gives me that *poor stupid girl* look again, and I let him. I take it because it's true. I *am* a poor stupid girl right now, a realization that makes me cry harder.

"It just means we've come full circle, Laila." His voice is dry. Emotionless. "We're back to where we started. Your family is on the top, and mine is on the bottom."

Darren Gansler's voice echoes through my thoughts. *I'm always on whichever side is winning.* And my mother's comment to him, just this morning: *You control the money, so you control the outcome, Darren.*

And I know that Amir is correct. That Mother has clawed her way back to the top, turning against Amir's family—and everyone and everything they represent—in the process.

"It's not right," I whisper.

"No, it's not." And this time, it's his hand squeezing mine. Amir shoves the envelope into his pocket as he stands up. He nods once, slowly, almost a bow, and then walks back into the restaurant without me.

FOCUS

I feel different when I wake the next day. Inside out. Raw.

I rise from bed and fumble through my morning routine. We have a routine now. How did I not notice this before? Mother heats the water. I set out the spoons. Bastien's job is less defined, but he is reliably watchful. More so than most boys his age, I think.

"Can I turn on cartoons?" He doesn't usually ask permission. Mother starts to shake her head but then glances over at me. I shrug in response.

We were up late watching the news again. Coverage of the fighting, already skimpy, had become nonexistent by the time we went to bed. The chance of an update is small, so Mother sighs her consent at Bastien and the room fills with the sounds of superheroes.

We eat breakfast without speaking, our lives guiltily unchanged by the war back home.

I still feel different when I get to school. No one else

seems to, though. "Laila, look at these pictures!" Emmy seems to have forgotten about our falling-out the day before; she joins me at my locker and hands me her phone so I can scroll through the digital photos someone sent her.

Who had a camera? I didn't notice anyone taking pictures in the park.

"You look beautiful." Emmy beams when I say this.

The photos are remarkable for their fiction. They tell a story of an entirely different day than the one I experienced.

"This one's my favorite." She scrolls to the last one. In it the sun appears to shine—the product of either a clever camera or a very brief break in the clouds, since I remember no bright moments like the one here. Emmy looks like pure joy in the image—her face, tilted back and laughing, shows no trace of disappointment or anger. Tori and Morgan are aware that a photo is being taken—they're making funny kissy faces at the camera. They're a photogenic team, vamping, giggling, and radiating an energy that spreads everywhere in the picture except to me. I am a faded blur, alone in the center of these happy, beautiful girls. My eyes are downcast, and my expression dour.

"You look so mysterious. Laila, our International Woman of Mystery!" As always, Emmy finds something kind to say. But behind her words I sense a new reserve—perhaps our argument hasn't been forgotten, after all. "The bell's about to ring—see you later." That she rushes off without concrete plans for lunch proves to me that all is not as it once was with Emmy.

"Bye," I say to her back.

I run my fingers along the wall as I walk to class, tracing a path. Holding on.

TRIGGER

It's dissection day in biology. Fetal pigs. Mr. Farleigh barks instructions over the jittery giggles in the room. "Three students to a pig, everyone. Do you hear me? Team up and have one person from each group grab your tools." Scalpels are strewn across a table at the front of the room. Forceps. Probes. A tray holds one spread-eagled specimen, already dissected. "This is what you will end up with if you follow my instructions." He's shouting now, his words nearly drowned out by the noise of twenty-four students vying for lab partners. I remain still. I'm the odd man out—silent number twenty-five.

Bacon jokes fly around the classroom, as do the predictable snorts and squeals. Besides me, only the actual pigs are quiet—they're pale and shriveled and peaceful.

Mr. Farleigh continues to yell over the noise, drill-sergeant droll. "Every year the district gets at least one complaint about this lab. If you are so inclined, listen carefully before you go running to Mommy and Daddy. I don't care if you're vegetarian. Or vegan. Or fruitarian—that's a real thing, I'm told. The school board has determined that this lab is a nonnegotiable requirement, no matter what crazy fad diet you may be following. You will complete this assignment, or you will fail this class."

But then his tone turns formal. Looking at me, only me, he speaks more quietly. "The only exception is for religious beliefs. If you object to handling the specimen on religious grounds, please come see me right away."

At first I'm confused. Up until that moment, I had been thinking the same thoughts as probably every other student in the class: *Ew. Gross. Cool.* Religion had never entered my mind. *Are Muslims not allowed to dissect pigs?* I had no idea. What about Jewish students? It's an interesting question—one I can take my time to ponder, since no one has chosen me for their lab group.

Something about it—about the question, about the day, about my life here—makes me laugh out loud. It's not a healthy sound. At first it's a hitching snort, but it quickly grows into a donkey's bray tinged with a hint of shriek, and I can't seem to stop. Soon the entire class is staring wordlessly at me.

I can't catch my breath.

Mr. Farleigh looks disgusted. He clearly thinks I'm just some stupid, squeamish girl hysterical at the thought of touching a pickled pig. But that's not it.

It's not the assignment—it's the moment. It's the quiet, pale faces clustered around me. It's the body on the tray, trussed and flayed. It's not having a lab partner. It's looking around, wondering who woke up yesterday morning in their peaceful suburban bedroom, picked up a phone, and called to report a bomb just for fun. It's me. Here.

I stand up and race out the door.

Because I cannot even flee a room without complications, I bump into someone in the process. "I'm sorry. Excuse me. Sorry." I should help him pick up the books I knocked out of his arms, but I don't. I don't know his name, this human obstacle standing between me and escape, and there's no point in learning it. There's nothing for me here, and I don't feel like pretending otherwise. My energy is gone, my strength nonexistent, and it's all I can do to just get out.

"Pardon me, young lady. You are not excused from class!" I ignore the teacher as he leans out his door to shout at me. There's no point answering him, no point turning back. *I do not belong here. There is nothing for me here.* This becomes my mantra as I escape.

The hallways feel foreign to me, stranger even than on my first day here. I'm running now, passing so many rooms I'll never enter filled with so many people I'll never speak to. I pass dusty trophy cases and endless rows of dented lockers. I'm almost at the big double doors, almost free, when I bump into the second person in as many minutes.

"Laila, stop. Are you okay?"

It's Ian of all people—a slap of a coincidence. Or perhaps no coincidence at all, since he always seems to be everywhere I am. "I'm leaving." I'm dizzy, gasping for air, but I manage to wheeze out what's already obvious: "I can't breathe."

He steers me to a stairwell and then helps me sit down. "Do you have asthma?" And then when I shake my head, "Are you maybe having a panic attack? I'm only asking because my mom gets them sometimes, and you look exactly like she does when she's having one. Your eyes, especially." He brushes a tear from the corner of my eye with a barely there touch as he says this.

I laugh the braying donkey's laugh again; the harsh sound echoes in the stairwell, making me clamp my mouth shut. *A panic attack?* What a luxurious problem to have. To be attacked by one's own panic rather than shot at, bombed, or gassed.

And yet, I *am* panicked. I *am* panicking.

Ian is talking to me in a low voice, telling me about some printing problem with this week's school paper. It's a boring, pointless story, but its value is in the telling, in the murmuring. I should be annoyed; he's trying to calm me the way you would a wild animal—a growling dog or a rearing horse. But I'm not annoyed, since it seems to be working. My galloping heart slows to a trot, and my fists unclench, my fingernails leaving purple-red grooves on my palms.

I hold up one hand. "Stop. It's okay, Ian. Stop. I'm okay now."

"Are you sure? Do you want me to get someone for you? The nurse? Wait, scratch that. I don't think we even have a school nurse. Do we?"

The tension snaps and fades, and I give him a tepid smile. "No, I'm really okay. Embarrassed maybe, but I'm fine." I feel watery-limbed and light-headed, but he doesn't need to know that.

"Has that ever happened to you before?"

"No," I lie. But it *has* happened. At the football game. At the school dance. Any time my past has collided with my present. Sounds and smells and memories from home might as well be bullets.

"Because I could talk to my mom about it, if you want. Find out how she deals with it. She does yoga and meditates sometimes, stuff like that, and she might have some other ideas."

"No. Please, just drop it." I know he's trying to help, but I'm so far beyond yoga, or scented candles, or whatever feel-good methods people use to calm their suburban anxieties. What tidy little pill could remove the fear of my entire family being killed? What amount of meditation could erase the memory of being hunted, a screaming mob outside the gates? How many long bubble baths would I have to take to forget the image of my mother staggering out of my father's study, covered in his blood?

No, my panic is real. It won't be erased or cured for all the yoga poses in the world. I must simply learn to absorb it better so that it doesn't leak out the way it has today.

"I need to go, Ian. But thank you. Really." I push myself up from the steps.

"Laila, you have people who care about you here. We want to help you, if you'll let us."

Those eyes. The way he looks at me, the way he is, I almost wish I could . . . I don't know what. I wish I could be the kind of person who could be with the kind of person he is. But I'm not. I shake my head once and then walk away from him one last time. He belongs to a different world now.

240

TIMING

The aftermath of a hurricane greets me when I get home. Mother has been busy.

Her box of secrets is open and scattered around the living room. Documents and maps are strewn across the coffee table, and confetti shreds of paper cling to the rug. My laptop sits on the kitchen counter, open to my email account. This surprises me—I didn't know Mother could turn on a computer, much less use one. I wonder briefly if *she* is spying on *me* just as I'm spying on her, but the thought is laughable. My life is not interesting enough to warrant her snooping. The most she'd see, if she cared to look, would be a few funny forwards from Ian and a handful of emails from Emmy complaining about teachers.

I have depressingly little to hide. Unlike her.

She has a guilty look on her face when I walk through the door. She too casually turns over the piece of paper nearest her and slips it to the bottom of a messy pile. "You're supposed to be in school." Her eyes are red.

"Yes." I look straight at her, silently daring her to ask more. Instead, her eyes skip over to the scene on the muted television behind me.

I try not to look, but I can't resist for long. There are more images from home dancing across the screen; boldface captions tell yet another gruesome tale. This time a lakeside resort has been attacked. The scene is familiar, both for the death and destruction I've grown accustomed to seeing and because I recognize the resort.

I've been there.

My grandmother—my mother's mother—took me there, perhaps three years ago, for One Last Vacation. I wasn't told about her cancer until the final day of the trip. "Three generations of women," my grandmother bragged to anyone who would listen. The resort was one of few destinations in my country for three women traveling alone. We weren't actually alone, of course—we had drivers and security guards, as always. But there was still something liberating about being in a place that was too exotic and too expensive for most people in our country. It was part of a Swiss chain, safe for its neutrality but considered scandalous because of the foreign journalists who kept the hotel booked year-round, along with a smattering of particularly adventurous German and Australian tourists. In their alien presence we allowed ourselves small acts of rebellion: a glass of sherry for Grandmother each afternoon, a leisurely, unveiled stroll for Mother, and a raucous game of badminton, played with a long-haired Dutch couple, for me. Such bliss!

And now it all lies in shambles—yet another blackened crater where there was once a peaceful refuge.

I raise the volume. *Retaliation for earlier attacks on the capital,* says the newscaster. *Government forces asserting control. A campaign to rid the country of foreign influence and illicit activities.* Tidy sound bites and anemic explanations blend together, while on-screen a stoop-shouldered man splashes bucket after bucket of water onto the red stains on the concrete veranda.

I silence the television again. I've heard enough.

Mother is still not dressed; her hair is still uncombed. She seems to compose herself later and later every day now. This, more than the scattered papers or the hijacked laptop or the medicinal-sweet smell of liquor that clings to her, worries me. My mother is many things, but sloppy is not one of them.

She's slipping, too.

"What are you doing?"

"I need to make a phone call." She sounds vague, as if the thought had just occurred to her. "What time is it?" She glances at her wrist, realizes she's not wearing a watch, and searches the walls for a clock. There are none. Not in this room, anyway, so she goes into the kitchen to check the display on the microwave. I know without looking that the numbers have been blinking, unset and ignored, since we moved in. Aside from the tiny alarm that sits at my bedside to wake me for school, none of us has much need for clocks. Our lives are divided into Before and After, and any further breakdown seems pointless.

Spotting my computer, Mother taps impatiently at the

space bar until the screen saver vanishes, then nods at the clock in the corner of the screen, satisfied. "Good. Not too late," she says under her breath, and then walks into her bedroom, cordless phone in hand, and shuts the door.

"Nice to see you too, Mother," I tell the door. "My day wasn't so great, but thank you for asking. Oh, and feel free to borrow my computer anytime."

I wait in the silence for one, two minutes before I creep over and nestle my ear against the door.

She's not using the speakerphone this time, but her curt familiarity gives her away and I know that it's my uncle on the other end. Again.

"That was a foolish mistake. Now is not the time to make the world your enemy—" There's a long pause before she continues. "It doesn't matter. How many foreigners died today? Ten? Twenty? It might as well be a thousand. The second you started attacking foreigners, you also started losing support. In fact, it might already be too late. Why would they give weapons to someone who is just going to turn on them—" She stops abruptly again, and I can practically hear him yelling through the receiver.

I trace question marks into the wall with my finger as I listen. Curving left to right, as the symbol appears in English, and then mirrored, right to left, a question from home. Even our punctuation marks are opposites—no wonder I can't fit comfortably here. I'm an Invisible Queen asking backward questions. The visual almost makes me smile: I'm a character who would do Lewis Carroll proud.

"The point is that it's now or never. If you wait any longer, the deal will be off the table." I can hear her footsteps on the other side of the door, pacing. Her voice grows louder. "No. It has to be *you*. I told you this already. I'm having enough trouble convincing him that *you* deserve the support; there is no way he's going to hand over this much money, this much equipment, to a stranger. There is too much at stake. It has to be you."

Another long pause. I hear her drumming her fingers on a hard surface, waiting her turn. "It's enough. More than enough. They think they're buying a new world order, after all. That doesn't come cheap." Her laugh is like sandpaper. "Two days. Maybe three. I'll send you the details, the way we discussed. . . . No, not now. . . . Because some things shouldn't be discussed over the phone. You of all people ought to know that." She's losing the battle to keep the impatience out of her voice, and after another pause she finally gives in to her anger. "How could I ever forget? You've made sure of that. But don't you forget *your* end of the deal, either."

A faint beep tells me she's hung up, so I scurry into the bathroom and lock the door. I need a reason not to be in the same room as her right now, so I turn on the shower and let the water run. It's loud enough, I hope, to cover the sound of my sobs as I mourn the complete loss of the woman I believed my mother to be.

DESCENT

I feel polluted. Tainted. Like one of those birds you see in photos every time there's a big oil spill. Scrawny-necked, limp-winged creatures smothering under blankets of thick black tar, always with that same hopeless look in their shock-deadened eyes—that *What the hell am I supposed to do now?* look.

I suspect I have the very same look. But in place of oil, I'm coated with greasy, suffocating layers of shame. Sticky self-loathing glues me in place as I stand outside the school. Across the street. As far away as I can be and still watch, still see the bouncy steps of everyone who isn't me entering the building.

From here they look like nondescript human-shaped bubbles: shiny and fragile and totally without substance. It's a mean, childish thought, I know, but watching them turns me spiteful. They're only bubbles when compared to tar-streaked, grief-tangled me. They live in a world in which there are no bloodstains upon the pavement and no gift-bearing spies. I would also float and glisten in such a world.

I hold in my hand as heavy a paper as ever existed. The numbers and letters on it might as well already be bodies. I'm holding a pen-and-ink graveyard.

I fold it carefully and tuck it into my pocket.

One full day has passed. Two are left. Two days to do nothing, or two days to do something.

I see Emmy approach, but she doesn't see me. I'm not hiding, but she's not looking. She's walking fast, a brisk, stiff-legged shuffle, less buoyant than usual. In her delicate bubble world, she has lost much. Her parents are divorcing. The charmed, photo-op love life she's created on her walls doesn't exist in real time, and her best friend has abandoned her. I am sorry for my role in this. I am sorry for her pain. But still I don't wave or call to her. I don't think of myself as superstitious, but it does seem as if my bad fortune has rubbed off on her. It's better for everyone if I keep my distance.

I don't see Ian. I'm not here to see him anyway, but a quick sighting would have been nice—a glimpse of something that almost was.

In a way, I'm saying goodbye. To my friends, to the school, to my life here. This was not my intention, but after the confrontation I had with Mother last night, it seems inevitable.

"I know what you're doing, Mother. I know what you're planning, and I think it's disgusting."

She'd stared at me for a long time before responding. "You know about your uncle, then." She sounded neither angry nor

247

surprised. She went back to stirring the soup reheating on the stove before continuing. "There's nothing to worry about. We have to start somewhere, and we might as well start at the top. *Someone* has to be in power if we're ever going to move forward."

As usual, her answer just made everything *more* confusing. "You're playing with people's lives."

"I'm not 'playing' anything. I'm taking charge of our lives. Of our future. It has to be done if we're to survive. Dammit, ouch!" She jumped away from the stove and ran her scalded finger under cold water from the sink. "Please, Laila, I can't talk about this right now. Just set the table and tell your brother that dinner is almost ready."

After that she seemed to shut off. Her face was a stiff mask, and over dinner we barely spoke. Even Bastien was quieter than usual, shrugging when I asked him if anything was wrong. He sensed something. He must have.

Sitting there in our tensely silent home, I decided to follow in my mother's footsteps. I decided to take charge.

It was easier than I thought.

I found her message later that night. Mother may know how to send an email, but she doesn't know enough to erase her tracks. Either that or she simply didn't care if I discovered her treachery.

It was there in my Sent folder—a message made up entirely of numbers, impersonal and ominous. Three strings of digits in three different configurations had been sent to a nameless recipient at an address also comprised of numbers: 8352_9@comsenet.com.

I studied the numbers, staring at them until they made sense. There was a date. There was a time. And there was a place. I recognized the geocoordinate format right away, but I plugged the sequence into Google Earth to be certain. I braced myself as I used shaky fingers to type in the numbers and then hit Enter, but the swooping results still turned my stomach. The image on the monitor pulled away from almost–Washington, D.C., zipped me into a satellite's view of the earth from outer space, and then plummeted down to a fuzzy new image that took too long to become clear, as if even the pixels were reluctant visitors to the place on the screen.

It was the location underlined in red in my mother's notes—the small turnoff from a twisty mountain road, probably two hours from the capital. It's isolated—a good spot for a secret meeting. I imagine that Mr. Darren Gansler is skilled at choosing just such places.

The fact that Mother had sent the message from *my* email account, with *my* name attached to it, made me queasy with anger. My stomach danced an oily revolt, and for a moment I thought I might vomit. I closed my eyes and took long, deep breaths until the feeling passed. I couldn't be sick. I had work to do.

I knew the when and the where. The why was still a mystery. I steeled myself, then sat down to use my blood-money computer and a wifi signal stolen from my neighbor to give me the answers that my mother would not.

During the night I became an expert in terrible, evil things.

I read the things I couldn't bring myself to read before— the words that had turned me fearful of libraries. Firsthand accounts I'd cowardly skipped. Pages I'd quickly closed.

I opened my eyes.

I learned about arms transfers and foreign policy and civil wars. I read about amnesty and tribunals, about prison conditions and mercenaries. Every article, every website, opened a new wormhole, and then another, and another. There was no end to what I didn't know, it seemed. I googled "torture" and immediately wished I hadn't.

I want to go back in time, to scour the words and the images from my mind. I wish to unsee what I have seen. But my brain keeps attacking me with what I have learned. I keep picturing Amir's father, who I imagine as an older, broader version of him. I see him in jail, and I see him suffer. I can't escape his pain.

At one point, late during the night, or perhaps very early in the morning, I looked over at Bastien sleeping soundly in his bed. He'd always been able to sleep through anything. But suddenly I wanted to wake him. I wanted him to get up, to tell me a silly story about his day at school or pester me to play basketball with him outside. I needed—*desperately* needed— some show of his sweetness. I needed proof that not everyone in my family was damned by the blood in their veins. That *I* wasn't damned.

I let him sleep. One of us should.

Now I wait, my eyelids heavy with fatigue and my thoughts scorched with guilt. No matter what I do next, I betray someone. The question is who.

I finger the paper in my pocket as I finally spot Amir walking toward the school.

I've made my choice.

OUTCOMES

I can't leave. I can't bear the thought that I might miss some-thing or even come back to find the apartment empty, my tiny, splintered family gone without me. My thoughts shift like a Rubik's Cube—countless configurations of people and events clicking and twisting through my head until I'm dizzy and then numb.

The school calls twice. Mother ignores the ringing phone, so I pick up and pretend not to speak English and they stop calling. It occurs to me too late that they might report my truancy, that it might impact our legal status here, and then my worries bloom and multiply. I can't move in any direction without risking disaster, it seems, so I sit as quietly as I can without moving, watching news reports that cycle through sporting events and political speeches and house fires and drug recalls and anything, it seems, except news from home.

Emmy calls once, too. It's loud in the background—she's

calling from between classes—and she's unusually aloof. She's being a friend without being friendly. "I'm just calling to check in. You haven't been at school for a couple of days, and Ian and I are worried about you." She can't maintain the icy stiffness, though, and a hint of warmth sneaks back into her voice. "Are you okay, Laila? I just don't understand."

I hear the question behind her question. "I'm sorry, Emmy. I just—" I pause. Try to think of a way to explain. But I can't. "There's just a lot going on here. At home, I mean. It's complicated. I'm sorry I haven't been a good friend lately."

She does not disagree with me. "Well, I just wanted to see if you were okay." I can barely hear her over the hallway noise. "Will I see you later?"

I smile at the generosity of her vagueness. "Yes. Later. Goodbye, Emmy." After we hang up, I play with scenarios in my mind. I tell her everything. Or I go to school and pretend nothing is wrong. Or I make up something completely false—some easy excuse for my distance lately. A dread disease, maybe, or a secret boyfriend. None of these scenarios play out well, though. It seems that I have never learned to be a true friend, and it's too late to start now.

Ian does not call. I wish he would. I'm glad he doesn't.

Mother is drinking tea again; her liquor bottles sit untouched in their cabinet. Her hands are shaky, and I wonder if the drinking was worse than I realized. Or maybe she's nervous too, for whatever mysterious reasons she has to be nervous. I suspect we both have plenty of reasons, shared and unshared. We move about in distant silence, as if we have invisible bumpers around us that keep us from getting too close. In our small apartment this isn't easy, and sometimes our efforts to avoid one another feel like an awkward dance. We're two caged animals only barely managing to resist the instinct to turn on one another.

Bastien is at school. Not long ago he would have begged to stay home with us, but not anymore. Today he slipped out the door five minutes ahead of schedule without needing a single reminder to brush his teeth or remember his math homework. He has become remarkably self-sufficient, and it bothers me that I can't pinpoint when this change came about.

The date and time sent from my email account have come and gone. Minutes pass, then an hour, then two. My thoughts circle and twist, cycling between hope and despair and then back again, while I wait.

I don't wait long. The news arrives in person, announced by sharp, angry knocks on the door.

I jump at the unexpected noise, my heart hammering in my chest, but Mother seems unsurprised. She stands slowly and takes a long moment to smooth her unwrinkled clothes and finger-comb her perfectly coiffed hair. She is regal. Calm. Unrushed by the impatient pounding.

But I see signs of tension that other people might not. I see the way her shoulders draw in and up. I see the way she pauses, hand on the doorknob, just long enough to take a deep, steadying breath before finally opening the door.

Mr. Gansler, fist still raised, looks as if he would like to knock again, only this time on Mother's face instead of a closed door. I'm confused by his presence; I feel like I'm looking at his ghost. *Isn't he supposed to be halfway around the globe?*

The meeting time was only hours ago—there's no way he made it there and back already. He's sweaty and disheveled, and he has on his war zone clothes—the cargo pants and desert boots he was wearing the first time I met him. He looks like a different person dressed this way, and I wonder just how many identities he has. How many secret lives he has to juggle, and who he is when he goes home at night.

"What the hell happened?" he roars as he pushes his way past Mother. She raises an eyebrow as he slams the door closed behind him, but she does not speak.

"What have you done?" he demands again. "I was on the plane, Yasmin. On the damn plane! They had to radio the pilot with the news. Ten minutes later and we would've been in the air." A ropy vein pulses at his temple. "It's a goddamn mess there. The whole country is falling apart."

Mother still hasn't moved from her place beside the door. She has a strange expression on her face—an odd sort of half smile. She's too calm.

Mr. Gansler sees this. "What did you do, Yasmin?" His voice is a growl. But it's the growl of a wounded, defeated dog—the face-saving growl of retreat, not attack.

"I did nothing, Darren. Nothing other than what we discussed. I sent the message exactly as you instructed me to do." Her voice is smooth and soft; she might as well be remarking on the weather.

"The meeting was supposed to take place tomorrow. *To-*

morrow! So tell me why the hell the General showed up at the site twenty-four hours early?"

Mother's eyes widen, and she seems to shrink. "The General? Alone?"

Mr. Gansler's face is twisted with confused anger. He knows she's done something, but he doesn't know what. That makes two of us. "Of course *the General.* Your brother-in-law. The new and now former prime minister. He showed up twenty-four hours early to an ambush. It was a damn bloodbath—it's all a goddamn disaster!"

Mother's face pales, but she regains her strange smile. She looks . . . relieved. "Oh dear," she says without a trace of regret in her voice. "I must have told him the wrong day. What a terrible mix-up."

"*Mix-up?* You're the one who told him to show up early?" Mr. Gansler is twitchy; he vibrates with rage. "And who else did you tell? How did the opposition know where to attack? Who did you tell, Yasmin?"

He's yelling so loudly that the next-door neighbor starts her familiar pounding on the wall. *Bangbangbang.* We all ignore it.

"I didn't tell a soul. You have my word, Darren. I relayed the message only to him. I even avoided saying it over the phone, just as you advised." She's looking directly at him, challenging him with her honesty. "I admit that I made an error. I've never been good with dates. But I had *nothing* to do with an ambush."

He stares at her for a long time, trying to find a crack, trying to find the lie in her words. They lock eyes, neither one willing to yield. Finally, Mr. Gansler does. He closes his eyes and pinches the bridge of his nose. He seems to sag, and he looks suddenly tired. "We'll find out eventually, Yasmin," he says. "This isn't over."

"But—" She stops herself, as if debating whether or not to speak. "But what happened? You said there was a . . . a blood-bath. What was the outcome?"

Her hands are clasped to her chest; her eyes are pleading and wide. Every inch of my mother, a woman who has never shown a moment's interest in religion, seems to be praying for a specific answer. She doesn't look to be breathing.

"He's dead." There's no emotion in Mr. Gansler's voice as he walks toward the door. "A lot of people are dead. There was nowhere to go. That's why we picked that spot, remember? There was nothing for them to do but shoot at each other until most of them were dead."

"Wait," Mother says, rushing over to put her hand on the door so that he can't open it. "Who else is dead? Besides him?"

He yanks the door open hard enough that she has to pull her hand away and step back. "I don't know. He brought people. They brought people. They shot at each other. The whole country has gone to hell. Does it even matter?"

He's already gone when she whispers her answer. "I suppose it doesn't." She closes the door gently, almost gingerly, and then sinks to the floor. She's so bloodlessly pale now I can hardly believe she's conscious. She slumps and drops her face into shaking hands. And then she begins to wail.

Great, gulping sobs shake her shoulders, and she's crying harder than I've ever seen anyone cry. Her pain sounds otherworldly. She is haunted—an unfamiliar portrait of despair.

I watch her, frozen in place. I have seen her glassy-eyed and covered with my father's blood. I have seen her chased from her own home. I have seen her threatened and struck. But I have never seen her like this. Like all the grief in the world has been bottled inside her, only to pour out now, all at once, in ugly, agonizing waves.

I understand nothing. Nothing at all. But that doesn't stop the tears from forming in my own eyes, from coursing down my face and splashing to the floor beside my sobbing mother. There are so many different possible explanations both for the news brought by Mr. Gansler and for her grief. But I can't think of a single one that doesn't call for tears.

GATHERINGS

It seems that the Invisible Queen has accidentally sparked a revolution.

Life speeds up around me. The phone rings and rings, visitors of all accents come and go, and only my mother stands still. She is the eye of the storm.

Before the storm began, before these loud visitors arrived with their unbelievable quantities of food and paperwork, she allowed herself exactly ten minutes of despair. At the height of it—or perhaps the depth of it—I started to worry. Surely no one could recover from this sort of grief. She sounded hysterical, like a wounded animal, and I was certain that she had lost herself, that it was all simply too much even for her. My pessimistic mind was already racing ahead with questions of what to do next, who to call, how to manage—if nothing else, the recent weeks have made me resourceful. But my concern was premature. After ten minutes she picked herself up off the floor, walked to the cabinet, and poured two glasses of Father's favorite Scotch.

I watched her, puzzled. Was she pouring a drink for *me*? In truth, I hoped so. I've never liked the taste of liquor, but in that moment I craved its blur. I needed the edges of life to soften. But the second glass wasn't for me. Instead, she raised it high above her head and whispered my father's name. Standing over the sink, she poured it down the drain in a long, steady stream—an amber waterfall of a toast. Her liquid tribute complete, she emptied the second glass in a single gulp, dropped the half-full liquor bottle into the trash, then walked over and pulled me into her arms. "The hardest part is over, Laila. The worst is over," she murmured into my hair, holding me so tightly that it ached.

I admit the embrace weakened me. I stood still and let my mind go blank while she held me, basking in a rare empty moment. For the first time in so many weeks, I did not wonder. I did not doubt. I was safe, and I was loved. Nothing else mattered.

But such moments never last, and now the storm has struck. The answers I have wanted for so long are blowing in, and from the conversations swirling around me, from the visitors who talk over and in spite of me, I finally begin to understand.

There's been a betrayal.

No. It's more than that. It's an infinity knot of betrayal—an endless loop of double crosses. It was a setup from the beginning, with my mother betraying Mr. Gansler in order to betray my uncle, who started all this by betraying my father. And let us not forget the crimes that took place closer to home: she betrayed *me,* tricking me into betraying *her.* It's a bottomless pit of treachery—a twisted tangle of deceit and lies.

"Laila, darling. I'm so very, very sorry," she'd said at the end of our embrace. "I couldn't do it any other way. It had to come from you." She pulled away from me then, a sad smile on her face as she smoothed my hair. "And I'm sorry to tell you, my love, but you are a terrible liar. Truly awful. Your face gives you away every time. I needed you to believe the story so that Amir would believe *you.*"

Corrosive guilt churns in my gut, and I taste stomach acid. Amir. I have also betrayed Amir. I fed him the poisonous information that was fed to me. The two of us are the lowest links of this wretched food chain, and together we have been deceived. I am suddenly desperate to find him—to put things right. But I'm not a fool. I know it's too late. He will blame me. *Of course he will.*

There *was* a meeting planned—that much was true. Mr. Gansler was to meet with the General, an unofficial rendezvous outside the capital, away from prying eyes. Money was to be handed over; weapons, too. It was an ugly move in an ugly game, prompted by the need to control a situation spiraling out of control. A civil war in an oil-soaked nation leads to an excess of interested parties, from profiteers to Peace Corps, and everyone in between. The General—my hateful, murderous uncle—was chosen to emerge the victor for no other reason than because he was already there. A cruel and lazy choice if ever there was one.

But Mother had other plans. Twenty-four hours before Mr. Gansler could buy himself a king, my mother moved the chess pieces. My uncle and the rebels were slid into place a day early. A "mix-up," claims Mother, though we all know better. One day before the money and the guns arrived, two groups faced off. My uncle and the opposition. They had allied once against my father. Now they stood as enemies.

Both sides wanted the treasure; both sides were willing to fight to the death.

And so they did.

Information comes in bursts. Television news reports are too slow for this crowd. Instead, cell phones ring and beep and twitter relentlessly; our apartment sounds like a cage full of robotic birds. *Who are all these people, anyway? Where did they come from?*

Actually, I know where they come from, even if I don't recognize their faces. The room is filled with the language of home, though it's a burbling stew of regional accents. The air even smells like home—the aroma of the food I can only look at, since I doubt I could keep it down. Here gather the expatriates. The escapees who wish to go home; people who, judging from their callused hands and weary faces, work very hard in exchange for their refuge here. The fact that most of them fled during my father's reign is lost on no one. In spite of the noise—festive raised voices when the incoming rumors are good, and low mutters and quiet curses when the rumors are bad—no one *really* talks to anyone else. Facts are exchanged and names compared, but loyalties and opinions are kept safely tucked away. There is an undercurrent of suspicion and fear. Among these people my mother rises. She is the center. *I* am ignored completely.

The mood changes when Bastien walks through the door. School is out, and the King has arrived.

Dear Bastien, small for his age and teetering under the mountain of his overstuffed backpack, enters the storm with a seven-year-old's snack-hungry eyes and secret-joke smile, and something happens in the room. People look up. Conversations pause. Cell phones go unanswered. Bastien grins at the crowd. He grins at the cookies. He drops his backpack near the table and grabs a handful of sweets—as far as he's concerned, this is a party. The crowd, shy at first, slowly circles him, then swallows him altogether.

I watch this happen from where I'm sitting, perched on the kitchen counter. Am I the only one who sees the lunacy in this? In the making of a child-king? But that is unmistakably what is happening.

"He's the one. You can see it already. Watch how everyone rallies around him." It's Mr. Gansler, whose true name no longer matters to me. He's a nonentity. A representer of interests. A deliverer of other people's messages and other people's money. After he left here, something—or someone—must have convinced him to return and act civil. He's changed back into his Washington clothes—he's one of only a few men wearing ties here, and he looks out of place.

"He's *seven*."

Mr. Gansler shrugs. "He has the right name. That's what matters there, even if it shouldn't. And as much as people hated the last guy, they already hate the General even more." Too late, it occurs to him whom he's speaking to, and he flushes

262

a little. "Sorry. But your father wasn't exactly winning hearts and minds at the end."

There's a long pause, and Mr. Gansler watches me watching Bastien. A combination of apology and pity lingers on his face. "You don't have to worry about him, Laila. Your brother won't actually be responsible for anything. He'll just be the person out front. The one smiling in the pictures and waving at the crowds. There'll be people behind him making all the decisions, doing all the work."

"People like you."

"And people like your mother." He lifts his hand and waves to her across the room. Her eyebrows pinch when she sees us. She doesn't like the two of us talking.

"And yet he'll be the only one with a big target painted on his back. For whenever *they*"—I gesture around the room— "decide that maybe someone else would be better. Or when one of our cousins, perhaps, decides that *he* wants a turn, or—"

Mr. Gansler holds up his hand to stop me. "Whoa. Easy there. I didn't plan for things to work out this way, remember? Putting a seven-year-old in charge of a country isn't my idea of a smart move, either. Even if it *is* just for show."

"Then why are you doing it? Why don't you pick someone else?" A deep-down, childish urge to kick him in the shins bubbles up and is slow to subside.

"It's not as easy as that. Your country may not elect its leaders, but the people need to at least *think* they have a say in the matter. Besides, just look at them." He tilts his head toward Mother, who has made her way over to Bastien. She stands behind him, resting a proud hand on his shoulder. They glow together, like they were born with some internal light switch that I was not. "They're naturals," Mr. Gansler continues. "Your mom is an impressive woman, Laila. She's a lying, manipulative—" He stops himself, and I pick up the faint scent of his drinking.

I nod, taking perverse pleasure in the fact that my mother could drive the CIA to drink. "Yes, she is."

"You know, it's not lost on me that she did me a favor. She didn't mean to, I'm sure, but she did." His tongue has been loosened by whatever last filled his glass. "Twenty-four hours later, and I would've been there too. And I probably would have died." He's matter-of-fact, like it's a risk he accepts every day. Or maybe he's just liquor-brave. Probably both.

"So what's next?"

My question makes him smile and shake his head. "Ask your mother," he says. "I'm going home. I'm tired."

He starts to push his way through the crowd, and I call out to him. "Mr. Gansler, wait!"

He turns and I hesitate. *How much, exactly, has he had to drink?* Only enough to make him human, I finally decide. "Can you give me a ride somewhere?"

He glances at my mother before answering me. Her head is pressed next to a stranger's—they're both listening intently to a cell phone that the man holds between them. Mr. Gansler sighs. "Sure. Come on."

Neither of us bothers to say goodbye before we slip out the door.

BLOWS

If Mr. Gansler recognizes the address I give him, he doesn't say so. In fact, he doesn't say anything at all during our short car ride together. He just sweeps the fast-food wrappers from the passenger seat before I get in. There's a child's booster seat and a healthy scattering of crumbs and broken crayons in the back—things that surprise me more than they should. The contents of his car are uncomfortably normal.

I start to thank him as I get out, but he waves me away. "I'll see you soon, Laila. Take care." He's robotic with exhaustion.

I'm wary as I walk up the steps of the building, but none of Amir's horrible neighbors are in sight. My stomach gurgles acidly as I knock on the door; it feels like a volcano is erupting in my belly. I can't remember the last time I ate.

A familiar man opens the door. He's been in our apartment before, and I remember him from Bastien's birthday party. I'm embarrassed that I don't know his name, but it seems too late to ask now.

He knows exactly who I am, though. I can tell from the way he looks like he wants to kill me.

For a long moment he just stares. "The doors of empty castles open wide," he says finally, in a hissing knife of a voice. It's an old saying from home that I've heard before, but it has never sounded so personal. Or so threatening. The man does not move aside. His hands open, then close into fists, and his nostrils flare. For a moment I think he's going to hit me. For a moment I *want* him to hit me, to substitute physical pain for guilt. *Do it,* I will him.

But he doesn't strike. "Amir!" He barks the name and whirls around, leaving the door to swing slowly shut.

As I wait awkwardly in the foyer, I realize that Amir's apartment is full of people, just like mine. But even through the closed door, I can hear a difference. The muted sounds *feel* different. I can hear a woman crying, and I know the gathering inside is not a happy one.

Finally, he comes to the door. Amir is dead-eyed and gray-faced, and he won't look directly at me. "You have some nerve showing up here." But his anger sounds anemic. Like he has no further energy to spare me—neither good nor bad. Like I am dead to him.

"Amir, I didn't know. I had no idea. I thought what I told you was true, I swear it." I know he'll hear my words as lies, but what else can I say?

He starts to close the door in my face, then changes his mind and swings it open so hard it slams against the wall.

Now, at last, he looks at me. It's almost comforting to see the hatred back in his eyes—it's better than the grieving nothingness of the moment before.

His voice is a barely controlled fury. "Our people showed up exactly where you told us. But you promised there'd be one man and enough guns and money to win the war. Instead, there were twenty men, no money, and the only guns were those in the hands of your uncle's supporters—the ones who ambushed our group. The ones who killed fifteen of my friends and relatives."

"Not your father . . . ?" I can only whisper my question, I want so badly for the answer to be no.

He doesn't reply at first, and I fear the worst. But then he shakes his head, a sideways tilt to his mouth making the scar on his cheek deepen and crease. "No, not my father," he finally says. "He's still recovering from his time in prison. Good thing, or he certainly would have been there. Tuberculosis and two bone fractures that were never properly set, and still my mother had to practically chain him to the bed to keep him from going. It's ironic, isn't it, that injuries from your father's people kept him from getting killed by your uncle's people?" He laughs in a way that isn't funny at all.

"I'm so glad, Amir. I was so scared—"

This was the wrong thing to say. He goes wide-eyed with incredulous anger and then grabs me roughly by the arm and pulls me into the apartment.

I could run away. I could push him, or yank my arm away, or scream for help. But instead, I let him pull me inside, half tripping as he drags me down the hallway into a crowded room. I'm limp with dread, and I let him shove me the last few inches. Dozens of eyes burn into me as everyone stops talking and turns to stare.

"You should know what you've done, Laila. There should be consequences. We did *your* dirty work. We killed your uncle, Laila. That's what you wanted, right?" His voice cracks, and he's breathing hard, but he isn't finished. "And let me guess. Right now people are coming out of the woodwork, gathering at your home, claiming they've supported your mother all along, even if just yesterday they were *here*, supporting *us*. Right? Your family wins again, Laila. It always does, doesn't it?"

I stand in the circle of judging, hating eyes, shrinking under the weight of Amir's accusations. His words feel like lash strokes, and it's all I can do to stay on my feet.

He's not finished. His voice grows quieter, thaws with compassion. But the compassion is not meant for me. "See her?" he asks, pointing to a middle-aged woman with anguished red eyes. "Her husband died. And him?" He spins and points to a young man who looks like a taller version of himself. "His father died." He singles out three more people. "And her, and him, and her? They all lost someone. Each of us did. Everyone in this room lost a friend, or a relative, or a neighbor, or . . ." A long-haired woman comes to his side and puts her hand on his shoulder, and he wilts.

"I didn't know," I whisper. I look at the floor, desperate to escape the stares. "I just thought—" I scramble for the right words, but they don't come.

Amir doesn't let me finish. "*I* just thought there was more to you. Something that could be trusted. But I was wrong. You *are* your father's daughter." He spits the last sentence, and from his mouth it sounds like a curse.

I'm hunched, cornered and cowed by the hate around me, and my mouth opens and closes uselessly as I realize there's nothing I can possibly say.

"Get out." The voice is thin and high, but unmistakably clear. *"Get out."* Nadeen, Amir's sister, repeats herself as she steps from behind a cluster of men and draws herself up to her full, crooked height.

I nod slowly and then turn to walk out, cringing as I wait for a blow that never comes.

No one else speaks. There is nothing left to be said.

POSSESSIONS

We've accumulated more than I realized since we arrived here. Mother and I stand together and fold, but already it's clear that much will be left behind.

"Should we keep these?" I ask, holding up a stack of Bastien's oh-so-American T-shirts. Skulls and crossbones; dinosaurs, monster trucks, and ninjas. Cheerful horrors adorn his wardrobe here.

"No." Mother shakes her head. "He won't need those." She retreats into her bedroom and then emerges with two familiar garments. She hands me one. "Will it be hard for you to go back to wearing this?"

I chew on my lip while I consider the veil. "No. I don't think so. It never really bothered me before, anyway."

She makes a face while she pulls her own veil up and over her hair. "I've always hated it." She tugs it off her head and tosses it aside. "Enough packing for now. Let's eat something."

But the cupboards are empty again. We're leaving tomorrow, and life has been too turbulent to think of things such as groceries. We sit at the table anyway, neither of us bothered by the lack of a meal. My stomach is too jumpy, my nerves too electric to eat.

"It's not going to be the same, Laila. You know that, right?" She's been gentle with me all week. Watchful, as if she's worried she has broken me. "The palace has been looted. Darren has only seen the outside, but he said it looks like there might have been a fire. There's probably nothing left inside."

When I don't say anything, she continues. "I just don't want you to be disappointed. I don't want you to expect things to be like they were before."

"I don't want things to be like before."

Mother tilts her head at this. Squints at me. So I repeat myself. "I won't do it. I won't go back to the way it was before. The lies. The betrayals. The violence."

Her eyes drop. We both know what I mean by this. For the first time, we both know the same things. "Your father—" she starts.

"Don't defend him!" I slap my hands down on the table. Hard.

She's still for a moment. Then she nods. "Your father loved us." Her voice is quiet.

"I know." On that one simple fact we can agree. The rest is too complicated and too painful to discuss now—or maybe ever. In order to go forward, much will have to remain unspoken. It's not forgiveness so much as it is . . . momentum. But I can't resist one last question.

"How did you know I'd do it? That I'd pass the information to Amir? That I'd even find it?"

Mother rises from her seat across the table. She comes around and sits in the chair next to mine, taking one of my hands in both of hers before answering. "Because you're *good*, Laila. Because you're smart, and decent, and kind. Not to mention terribly nosy and a shameless eavesdropper." She smiles at that, and her hands rise to stroke my hair. With featherlight fingers she turns my face toward hers so that I have to look at her as she speaks. "I didn't plan it this way. I didn't want to involve you. But you kept seeing what I hoped to keep hidden, and you kept hearing what I wanted kept secret. You learned things I wanted to protect you from, and then it was just too late. You were already involved."

She kisses my forehead and then sits back. "It's for the best, really. You were the one who could be trusted. By me, and by your friend Amir." She sees the argument on my face and continues quickly before I can interrupt. "I know he doesn't think so, and I'm sorry for that. Maybe someday he will. Probably not. But you saw something wrong, and so you did something right. You chose the only goodness you could see. Just like I knew you would."

She stands up slowly, kisses me one more time on the top of my head, and then walks back to the piles of clothing and starts to fold again. "Let's finish here. Tomorrow will be busy." She begins to hum a tune.

PATIENCE

She thinks it's over. She's been tiptoeing, waiting for me to rage and scream. To demand answers. To erupt. And now, after a two-minute conversation, she thinks the time for that has passed.

But it's not over.

My way is quieter. More fitting of an Invisible Queen.

VOID

Before I paid it a second visit this morning, the box under her bed contained more than just the geocoordinates. There were other numbers in there, too. Mother will discover their absence soon. Her folding, sorting, and packing should lead her there within the hour.

"I'm going for a walk," I call as I'm already halfway out the door. It's better if I'm not there when she finds what I've done.

REVERSAL

The photo jumped into my thoughts last night as I drifted off to sleep. So did a memory of Mother complaining about it during an afternoon visit to Father's office years ago. The memories were gifts from my subconscious, I think. Peace offerings from my troubled mind.

"Darling, really?" Mother had sighed as she plucked the photo from his desk. "This is hardly the best picture of us from our wedding. I look cross-eyed, and your hair looks a little thin from this angle, don't you think?" She'd reached over to fluff his hair playfully.

Father pulled her into his lap, spinning them around in his chair and making her shriek with laughter. An aide walked out, frowning his disapproval. My parents didn't care. For all their crimes, they did at least love one another.

"Someday, when we're old and wrinkled, my dear, you will look at this picture very differently. Your crossed eyes and my bald spot won't matter a bit to you then." He eased her from his lap with a kiss, then glanced at his watch. He was late for a meeting; it was time for us to go.

It was a touching moment, perhaps. But I know my mother's vanity. Choosing that photo, of all the more flattering photos she could have brought with her, made little sense. And I was quite certain the picture, in that ugly, distinctive frame, had always sat in Father's office, so how could she have it here with her now? When we'd had only minutes to grab what few possessions we could from our home? And why was it hidden under her bed, instead of displayed somewhere?

My father's words took on new importance in my sleep-fogged thoughts, and my brain began to tease apart the mystery. *Someday you will look at this picture very differently.*

He'd been under house arrest those last few days. I didn't know that until I read about it here. Not that it mattered much—as crafty as he was, I have no doubt he'd found some way to arrange for sensitive documents and important personal effects to be brought to him at home. The week before he died had been full of nervous visits from anxious men. Did one of them bring the picture as one last favor?

Why?

There was only one way to know. So this morning, while Mother showered and Bastien slept, I pulled the photo from the box.

Pulled the picture from the frame.

And studied the writing, my father's cramped and slanted scrawl, on the back.

*   *   *

Four.

It's the number of bank accounts in exotic destinations. Macao, which I'd never heard of. The Cayman Islands, where my parents vacationed once. Belize. They'd traveled there, too. Andorra. Duty-free shopping, Mother used to claim of her frequent visits. The internet connects the dots for me, tells me what these places have in common: offshore banking.

On the back of my mother's cross-eyed wedding-day face are routing numbers and passwords. Wiring instructions and sums. Dollar signs. Pounds.

Hundreds.

It's the number of years we could live like royalty if the account balances in Father's handwriting are true.

Contact information for three shell companies and two law firms completes the list. Important numbers, indeed. I don't know why Mother hasn't called them yet. I don't have *all* of the puzzle pieces.

Perhaps she was waiting until she thought no one was looking. A treasure this grand would certainly be worth suffering through a few months of empty cupboards.

But she waited too long.

The frame sits empty now in the box beneath the bed. The picture of my parents smiling in better days—even without the numbers on the back, it would be far too valuable a thing to risk losing. I fold it small and tuck it into my bra. I need to feel it against my skin.

Now *I* control the money.

I control the outcome.

I've learned my lessons well. I won't be betrayed again.

PROMISE

"Is that it? Is that one our plane?" Bastien races to the window and presses his face against the glass.

My brother is the King of Somewhere.

He's not a real king, and it's not a real place. It's a scorched and broken void, our Somewhere, but even that is better than nowhere at all. There's hope in Somewhere. Possibility.

Mother and Mr. Gansler are bickering on the other side of the room. She doesn't trust him, and he doesn't trust her.

They're both right.

I sit down on the hard plastic bench in the empty departure lounge. It's aggressively uncomfortable, an ode to a hasty departure.

I'm leaving behind a fairy tale—this land of plenty, so free with laughter and caresses. People like Emmy who give and give and give for no other reason than the pleasure of friendship. College loans and Happy Meals. Disneyland. Free re-

278

fills. Boys like Ian, with dazzling eyes and kind, good hearts. Librarians with arms full of books for the taking, and shiny plastic jewels. Picnics in the park. Lucky Charms.

So much happy artifice. Such fanciful illusions.

For me, these things will never be real.

My old life, the one I fled, *was* real. It *is* real. It is real pain, and real war, and real deaths, and real guns. I can't say that I'm excited, or happy to return. I'm not. What I am is *ready*.

I thought I was drowning here at times. But I wasn't. I was changing. In the moment, they feel the same. Equally traumatic. Equally permanent. But these breathless, underwater months here have cleansed us, I think. Left us less singed than when we arrived. We are ready, the three of us—ready to go *home*. Ready to do whatever it takes to transform our Nowhere into something beautiful and peaceful.

Ready to make amends.

The edges of the folded picture dig into the skin near my heart. It's my insurance policy. My weapon. My treasure. When the time comes, I will be happy to let it go. I have people and places I can hardly wait to visit. I'll leave a bit of the treasure wherever I go—a merry trail of golden crumbs. Perhaps my homeland can produce a happy fairy tale yet.

Mother knows.

We don't discuss it. We won't discuss it. She looks at me differently now, with wary resignation on her face. She is at peace with my treachery. Or so she seems to be.

Really, only time will tell.

While we wait, I compose a farewell in my head. Dear Ian. Dear Emmy. Separate messages, of course, but both will contain the most important thing I have to say: Thank you. Thank you for giving me this in-between space in my life. The time and the place that rest between my Before and my After. It wasn't meant to be forever, I know that now, but thank you for embracing me as if it were.

I stop when I notice the sound of music playing overhead. It's Muzak—the watered-down version of a catchy song I heard Bastien singing along with just days ago. It will do. "Bastien," I call out. "Listen!"

His face lights up, and I stand, hold out my hand. We used to do this back home, back before everything crumbled. He looks sheepish, since seven *is* so much more mature than six, but he humors me and takes my hand. We dance a foolish, spinning dance together, and I catch our reflection in the glass. There's me, hair streaming, head unveiled, and there's Bastien, a grinning, spinning, laughing child. I file the images away in my mind; they won't be seen again.

"Okay, that's enough, you two." Mother is smiling as she claps her hands at us. "It's time to go."

I linger only slightly before I follow them to the boarding gate. I take one last breath, filling my lungs with the air of this place, and I make one more silent promise to myself. I am my mother's daughter. I am my father's daughter. And I have learned from their mistakes.

I am the Invisible Queen.

AUTHOR'S NOTE

The seed for this story was planted years before I started writing it.

I spent the summer of 2003 in Baghdad, Iraq. Saddam Hussein was on the run, leaving behind a jaw-dropping collection of opulent properties. My work at the time took me through some of his palaces—some intact, some heavily shelled, and all thoroughly looted.

One of the compounds had housed various relatives, including a number of young children. On the property was a kids' playhouse built into the side of a hill, though "playhouse" doesn't even come close to describing the elaborate faux-rock structure. It was as if the Flintstones had built a Stone Age palace—an enormous multilevel maze with built-in seats and tables, an intercom system, and stereo speakers installed in most rooms. There was even an elevator. It was pure excess and was no doubt thoroughly enjoyed by whoever had played there.

Who were these children? I wondered. Did they know the secrets of the man who had built this palace of a playhouse? Did they realize how different their lives were from those of other children in their country? Was Saddam Hussein just a friendly grandfather/

uncle/godfather to them? When they came of age and learned more, were they shocked?

The idea behind the book didn't crystallize for another seven years. I was a mother by then, and had just moved onto a military base with my family. Various loud military exercises were a part of life there, and it was months before I stopped jumping every time I heard an explosion. My young son adapted far more quickly, and one day, not long after we had arrived, I was taken aback when he responded to the sound of gunfire by asking me to turn up the volume so that he could hear his Nemo video over the noise. His reaction rattled me. *What type of life leads a child to find the sound of gunfire nothing more than a distraction from a cartoon?* I asked myself. And in that moment—in that question—Bastien's character began to grow.

When I finally began to write the story, I did not want Laila and Bastien's home country to be a thinly disguised version of any one particular place—Iraq, or elsewhere. To avoid this, and to avoid the trap of having to be too wed to actual events, I created a melting pot of details, current events, and personal experiences.

I started writing in 2011, a year or so into the Arab Spring movement that was bringing so many changes to the Middle East and North Africa. What began as a smattering of local disputes had spread like wildfire, crossing borders and tapping into deep veins of civil unrest. Before long it escalated into a wave of protests, uprisings, and civil wars. The whole region seemed to be rising up against the authority of repressive regimes, calling out human rights abuses and condemning the leaders who had allowed inequality to fester and grow. On top of that, the continued presence of the U.S. military in the region added yet another layer of turmoil. At times the sheer volume of pertinent material appearing in the media seemed eerie—almost as if the news was writing my story along with me:

- After being ousted from office and with his palace surrounded, the president of Tunisia fled the country with his wife and three children. He and his wife were both convicted in absentia of various crimes.
- Osama bin Laden was found living a cloistered existence in Pakistan; no one knew what to do with his wives and children after he was killed. Were they innocents? What did they know? Where should they go?
- Rulers were being forced from power in one country after another: Egypt. Libya. Mali.

As I wrote, the daily news brought me inspiration from other parts of the world as well—for example, when Kim Jong-un, still in his twenties and completely without leadership experience, was declared North Korea's supreme leader after his father's death. He wasn't exactly a seven-year-old king, but I couldn't ignore the parallels.

And then came Syria. Any time I began to worry that my plot was becoming melodramatic (*Was a school bombing perhaps too much for this sort of a book? The memory of a body in the street too sensational?*), painful images from Houla, Homs, Ghouta, and Aleppo told me that my plot didn't even scratch the surface of the atrocities happening in the world every day.

Similarities between what my characters were going through

and real-world current events sometimes chilled me. Days after I wrote the scene in which Laila watches the news of a bombing at a vacation locale, for example, twenty people died in Afghanistan when a lakeside resort was attacked. I grimly went back and changed my mountain retreat to a lakeside resort in the text.

But the overlaps between what I wrote on one day and then read in the news the next were not eerie coincidences. I was simply paying more attention to the terrible things that appear in the news every day, because my characters were making those tragedies more personal.

Ultimately, this book is pure fiction that is inspired by real events. It isn't about a specific conflict any more than it is about any one particular country. Rather, it's the personal story of someone living on the periphery of war. It's the story of a girl grappling with questions about guilt, choice, blame, and identity under circumstances both extraordinary and mundane. It's a big story told in small details, and I hope that my readers come away feeling as if faraway issues are now a little more personal.

TRUTH IN FICTION

A Commentary by Dr. Cheryl Benard

Some years ago, I had the opportunity to interview Benazir Bhutto. Benazir was more than just a newsworthy personality to me; I had followed her life and career with fascination for many years. Her father was Zulfikar Ali Bhutto, the heir to a powerful land-owning family and founder of the Pakistan People's Party (PPP). Zulfikar was British-educated, handsome, and stately, a glittering figure who rose swiftly to power as the head of his party and then president and prime minister of Pakistan. His fall from grace, however, had been even more dramatic; he was overthrown by a military coup and jailed on charges of ordering a political assassination. Even as the international community vociferously protested what it said were trumped-up charges, he was hanged without a proper trial.

J. C. Carleson's book builds on the observation that political personalities of all stripes—dictators, megalomaniacs, patriotic heroes—have families and friends who, in turn, have hopes, dreams, fears, and ambitions that lead them to take actions, or to refrain from taking actions, with the potential to change the course of history. That may seem like a simple premise, but the path from premise to understanding is lengthy and, I submit to you, as yet unexplored in the study of politics. It's like saying "germs cause disease." Right, but that puts you at the beginning, not the end, of your medical quest.

Benazir was her father's first and favorite child, and his anointed successor. She was just twenty-five when he was imprisoned and sentenced to death by a kangaroo court; she threw herself into the effort to save him, filing petitions with the courts, mobilizing international support and protests and requests for clemency by foreign heads of state. After his execution, the entire family, including Benazir's brothers and her mother, was jailed by the military government; Benazir spent years locked up under harsh conditions, including solitary confinement in a cage-like prison in a remote desert province. Her brothers joined extremist groups. One became a terrorist; both ultimately died young—one of poisoning, the other in a shoot-out with police. Benazir, meticulously educated abroad like her father, a graduate of both Harvard and Oxford, took up her father's mantle. At twenty-nine she was proclaimed the new head of the PPP. Six years later, she was elected prime minister of Pakistan, one of the world's most turbulent, conservative, and patriarchal nations. Her election campaign produced electrifying images of a slender young woman, poised, confident, articulate, addressing crowds numbering in the hundreds of thousands who cheered hysterically as she promised them that she would fight for them and for social justice and education and freedom. My feminist heart had been thrilled.

But it had all gone downhill from there, steeply. Instead of leading her nation to stability and prosperity, she had become embroiled in scandal. Both her terms of office had been cut short. She had married a man whose nickname was Mr. Ten Percent, because that was the cut he allegedly required before his wife would sign off on any major national business deals. He had been jailed for financial wrongdoing, corruption, and possible involvement in political murders. She had been forced to flee the country to avoid being put on trial herself, and all her energies now went into getting her husband out of prison and proving his innocence. It seemed like a tragic waste.

So when I met her in Washington, D.C., many years later, I threw all of this on the table. I figured I had nothing to lose; the worst she could do was get angry and order me to leave. Instead, she was silent for a few minutes. And then she agreed with me. Yes, she said, that was exactly how she felt about it, too. She hadn't just failed the women of the world and the people of her country; she had disappointed herself. And she had thought long and hard about the reasons for her failure. "You know," she said, "my father set me on the course of a political career. I was educated for it in some of the world's top schools. I learned everything there was to know about international relations, economics, political science. And when I returned to Pakistan, it took me just a few days to realize that nothing I had been taught had the slightest application to the way politics actually worked in my country." There, the only thing that counted was her father's cronies pulling the strings, ensuring that this young woman remain a sentimental figurehead for the party and nothing more. The only way to get anything done was through the tangled network of relationships and bribes and threats and favors that was the actual motor of Pakistan's political system.

She had been completely caught off guard by this, and by the time she had started to figure things out, she was already out of office. Her second term didn't really count, she said; they had gotten rid of her after just a few months, before she could initiate any kind of action. But this time, she told me, the next time, the third time, she would be prepared. She was a mature woman now. She had spent decades forging her own networks and alliances, across the Middle East and in Europe and the United States. I was disarmed by her candor, taken aback by this glimpse behind the scenes. In the years that followed, we spent time together regularly, in small social settings where she could let her guard down and reveal her hopes and suspicions and her vision.

In 2007—we had become friends by then, and I was rooting for her—she returned to Pakistan once more to run for the office of prime minister in an election everyone agreed she was certain to win. And this time, she felt ready. She had survived jail, house arrest, and exile. She had the masses behind her. The young people loved her. She had powerful supporters in the West and in the Arab world. She had smart advisers. She wasn't going to play the Pakistani establishment's game this time around, and she wasn't a young girl anymore, easy for them to control.

So they killed her.

And that's not just my personal suspicion—it's the finding of the official United Nations commission that was sent to look into her assassination. It was a few weeks before the election, which by all accounts she was a shoo-in to win. She gave a campaign speech, and at its conclusion, as she waved to the cheering crowd, an assassin fired two shots from his pistol and then detonated his suicide belt. The escape route previously prepared by her security team was unaccountably blocked by Pakistani police vehicles. The second car, the companion vehicle that is always supposed to remain directly in front of or behind the VIP vehicle for just such emergencies, sped away and left her. Her driver heroically tried to get her to a hospital, bumping along the public road in a vehicle with four blown-out tires. Halfway there, it broke down completely; Benazir was transferred to the private car of a friend who had sped after. At the hospital, she was pronounced dead. Since it was clearly an assassination and many questions were sure to be asked, the doctors urged an autopsy. Pakistani authorities forbade it, and instead whisked the body away to a military facility. Within hours, Pakistani police had hosed down the entire crime scene, making any collection of evidence impossible. But was it ineptitude or a cover-up? And her father, the great Zulfikar Ali Bhutto—was he a political visionary or a murderer, as his accusers alleged? What about Benazir herself? Was she an idealist or just trying to fatten up the family's Swiss bank account with another round of ten percents? And her husband, who became prime minister in her stead—was he a grieving, loyal widower or an ambitious operator who may have been complicit in her murder? All of the above represent views strongly held by different factions. Which version is true? None of them. All of them.

Benazir had told me that her fancy Ivy League education didn't help one whit in the real world of Islamabad intrigue. In the halls of academe, she had immersed herself in compelling, complex, logical schools of thought—but on the ground, what she encountered was messy, murky, cruel, dirty, and random. She is certainly not the first or the only one to take note of this. The Afghan political activist Meena, a charismatic woman who led a resistance movement during the 1980s and built a network of girls' schools and orphanages along with her own political party, had a similar observation.

"Politics," she said, "is an animal, a wild, wild animal." That came true for her; she was assassinated at the age of thirty. Like Benazir, I too studied political science and international relations, and my life has kept me close to the pulse of current events, though thankfully as an observer and not a participant. For me, the biggest surprise has been the role played in world affairs by personalities, relationships . . . and sheer random coincidence. In the textbooks, it all sounds so weighty and so rational, as though it were all about socioeconomic conditions, the spread of new ideologies, revolutionary eras, and waves of migration. But the realities of political life are chock-full of the human factor in all of its trivial, lowly messiness. Greed. Rivalries. Arrogance. People who keep critical information from each other, information that could save thousands of lives, just because they don't like each other or don't want someone else to get the credit. Betrayal committed just because someone felt slighted. Presidents who watch helplessly while their relatives rob the country blind, sabotaging the nation-building effort by diverting billions into their own pockets; presidents who can order an army into war but don't feel able to stand up to their older brothers. Previously forceful leaders who suddenly panic and flee in the face of a manageable uprising, and later it is revealed that they were in the advanced stages of cancer and had lost their will and confidence.

I am not denying that history can change course because of informed decision making, but don't underestimate the ability of a few greedy, jealous, ambitious individuals to give history's course a twist as well. And it's not just the bad motivations of selfish people or the misguided notions of fanatics that we have to worry about. Even where motives are pure—arguably a rarity when it comes to human beings—the results can be disastrous. Because the problem with good intentions is that, in the absence of perfect information, you cannot be sure of the consequences of your intervention. The road to hell is paved with good intentions, the saying goes, but I think that's much too glib. Let's amend it: The road to hell is paved with tiny, reasonable, apparently sensible compromises. It is paved with minuscule, forgivable human impulses and emotions that can cause utter havoc nonetheless. Read Montesquieu, read Etzioni, read Machiavelli, read Tocqueville. But you will learn more from the dramas of Shakespeare.

I love J. C. Carleson's book, but it's frightening—or maybe *haunting* is a better term. We see the world through the eyes of a young girl—bright, innocent, good-hearted, inquisitive, and sharply observant of the adults around her, as young people often are. Utter biographic circumstance has deposited her in a family that belongs to the Third World political elite, with all the luxurious benefits, deadly risks, and, perhaps worst of all, seductive temptations that implies. She loved her father, and maybe there was a part of him that deserved her love. After all, nothing is black-and-white. It's not even gray. It's a fractured, fragile kaleidoscope of colors ready to shift at the slightest nudge of the wheel. Good people can do bad things. Good people can do good things that turn out badly. Or they can do great things that shine like beacons for centuries to come. Bad people can do bad things that turn out well, or they can do terrible things that cause enormous misery. Or other people can do things intended to please the good or bad leader that he or she would not have endorsed. And whether you think that someone is a good or bad leader and that their actions were necessary or contemptible depends on who you are and whether or not your group benefited. And the judgment can change, sometimes from one day to the next, sometimes after a few centuries. Genghis Khan, for example, may be notorious for looting and killing, but today he is also credited with ushering in an era of unprecedented cultural exchange, peace, and prosperity.

I wish I could end on a "Yes, Virginia, there is a Santa Claus" note. I wish I could point to some core of certainty, some infallible set of ethical guideposts, but really all we have is questions. What, for example, will become of our young narrator? Will she hold on to her sympathy for the underdog and her inclination to fairness? And will she be able to convert that into any sort of effective action? Or will she fall into a life of comfort and privilege, paid for with ever more unsavory compromises? Asma al-Assad, the wife of Syrian dictator Bashar al-Assad, was once hailed by *Vogue* magazine as the "rose of Damascus" and praised for her work on behalf of women's rights and education. A few short years later, she was internationally reviled for standing by a husband who was allowing his population to be slaughtered in the streets. Her emails were hacked, and she was labeled a Middle Eastern equivalent of the frivolous Marie Antoinette when it became known that while battles raged in her country's cities, she was busy ordering shoes online.

What path shall we recommend to our heroine? Should she join the resistance? They resort, too often, to terrorism, convinced that the end justifies the means. Should she become a reformer? They often end up as political prisoners, rotting in dank, dark cells, but yes, others endure and become Nelson Mandela. Should she try to stay on the margins, because politics is just too confusing? A young woman named Sonia tried that route. Sonia was born in a small Italian village and received a strict Catholic education. To support herself while attending school, she worked as a waitress, and one day in came a strikingly handsome young man. They fell in love and got married. The man happened to be a student from India. He also happened to be the son of Indira Gandhi. But that, they both thought, mattered little. The young man, Rajiv Gandhi, was studying to become a pilot. He hated politics. His brother, Sanjay, was the one destined to lead the dynasty. Indira liked her foreign daughter-in-law, who was low-key and undemanding and whose principal involvement in family affairs was when she helped select the sari her mother-in-law should wear from a plenitude of gorgeous fabrics. Those moments brought them close. Then Indira was assassinated. And then Sanjay died in a plane crash. That left Rajiv, who was pressed to accept his fate and fulfill his duty to family, nation, and political party. He submitted, and became prime minister. And then *he* was assassinated. That left Sonia, who was now prevailed upon to step into her husband's shoes. Go to Wikipedia if you don't believe me; that's what happened. That's the crazy, completely unforeseeable chain of events that took an Italian village girl and made her leader of the biggest political party of Asia's largest democracy. *Forbes* has ranked her as the ninth most powerful person in the world.

So our young protagonist may try to enter the fray, or she may try to stay on the margins, but politics is a wild animal, and also a roller coaster without seat belts or rails, so we'll have to wait and see.

Dr. Cheryl Benard is a researcher for the RAND Corporation and president of ARCH International, a nonprofit organization dedicated to the support of post-conflict cultural activism. Previously she was the research director of the Ludwig Boltzmann Institute of Human Rights, a European think tank, and prior to that she taught political science at the University of Vienna.

RECOMMENDATIONS FOR FURTHER READING ON THE MIDDLE EAST AND THE ARAB SPRING

FOR YOUNG READERS

Children of War: Voices of Iraqi Refugees by Deborah Ellis

Tasting the Sky: A Palestinian Childhood by Ibtisam Barakat

Thura's Diary: My Life in Wartime Iraq by Thura al-Windawi

Sold by Patricia McCormick

Shabanu: Daughter of the Wind by Suzanne Fisher Staples

If You Could Be Mine by Sara Farizan

The Things a Brother Knows by Dana Reinhardt

Habibi by Naomi Shihab Nye

The Space Between Our Footsteps: Poems and Paintings from the Middle East by Naomi Shihab Nye

FOR ADULT READERS

Persepolis: The Story of a Childhood by Marjane Satrapi

Foreigner by Nahid Rachlin

The Kite Runner by Khaled Hosseini

Reading Lolita in Tehran by Azar Nafisi

Kabul Beauty School by Deborah Rodriguez with Kristin Ohlson

Arab Spring Dreams edited by Sohrab Ahmari and Nasser Weddady

The Arab Uprisings by James L. Gelvin

Veiled Courage: Inside the Afghan Women's Resistance by Dr. Cheryl Benard

ONLINE RESOURCES

While these books are all great resources, it's important to note that international affairs are in a constant state of flux. Situations can shift and evolve dramatically from year to year or day to day. The best way to stay informed is by reading the news. Here are a few websites that not only report current events but also offer historical overviews to put the headlines in context.

BBC News bbc.co.uk/news/world/middle_east

The New York Times nytimes.com/pages/world/middleeast
/index.html

The Guardian guardian.co.uk/world/interactive/2011/mar/22
/middle-east-protest-interactive-timeline

The Economist economist.com/world/middle-east-africa

CIA World Factbook cia.gov/library/publications/the-world-
factbook

J. C. Carleson

is a former undercover CIA officer who has navigated war zones, jumped out of airplanes, and worked on the front lines of international conflicts. Now a full-time writer, she lives in Virginia with her husband and two young sons. Her previous books include the novel *Cloaks and Veils* and *Work Like a Spy: Business Tips from a Former CIA Officer*. Visit her on the Web at JCCarleson.com.